The
ESSENTIAL COLLECTION

The

ESSENTIAL COLLECTION

#1 *New York Times* Bestselling Author

DEBBIE MACOMBER

A Friend or TWO

H HARLEQUIN®
™ESSENTIAL DEBBIE MACOMBER COLLECTION

Recycling programs
for this product may
not exist in your area.

ISBN-13: 978-0-373-47301-4

A FRIEND OR TWO

Copyright © 1985 by Debbie Macomber

For questions and comments about the quality of this book, please contact us
at CustomerService@Harlequin.com.

Printed in U.S.A.

DEBBIE MACOMBER

is a number one *New York Times* and *USA TODAY* best-selling author. Her books include *1225 Christmas Tree Lane, 1105 Yakima Street, A Turn in the Road, Hannah's List* and *Debbie Macomber's Christmas Cookbook*, as well as *Twenty Wishes, Summer on Blossom Street* and *Call Me Mrs. Miracle*. She has become a leading voice in women's fiction worldwide and her work has appeared on every major bestseller list, including those of the *New York Times, USA TODAY, Publishers Weekly* and *Entertainment Weekly*. She is a multiple award winner, and won the 2005 Quill Award for Best Romance. There are more than one hundred million copies of her books in print. Two of her Harlequin MIRA Christmas titles have been made into Hallmark Channel Original Movies, and the Hallmark Channel has launched a series based on her bestselling Cedar Cove series. For more information on Debbie and her books, visit her website, www.debbiemacomber.com.

In memory of Darlene Layman
Encourager and dear friend

Prologue

"Miss Elizabeth?" The elderly butler's eyes widened, but he composed himself quickly. "This is a surprise. Welcome home."

"Thank you, Bently. It's good to *be* home." Elizabeth Wainwright felt comforted by his formality and British accent. She looked around the huge entry hall, with its elegant crystal chandelier and imported oriental rugs and sighed inwardly. Home. Would it offer her what she hadn't been able to find in Europe? Immediately doubts filled her.

"Would you see to my luggage?" she asked in a low, distracted tone. "And ask Helene to draw my bath?"

"Right away."

She looked around with a renewed sense of appreciation for everything this house represented. Wealth. Tradition. Family pride. With all this at her fingertips, how could she possibly be dissatisfied?

"Bently, do you know where Father is?"

"In the library, miss," he responded crisply.

Her smile faded as she started across the huge hall. She loved Bently. Nothing could ruffle him. She could recall the time… Loud voices drifted past the partially opened door, and she paused. Her father rarely raised his voice.

"I'm afraid I've failed her, Mother. Elizabeth is restless and unhappy."

Stunned, Elizabeth stood just outside the library door, listening.

"Give the girl time, Charles. She's suffered a great loss." Her grandmother's raspy voice sounded troubled, despite her words.

"She has no drive, no ambition, no purpose. Dear heavens, have you seen these bills from Paris?"

The sound of his fist against the desk shocked her.

"Elizabeth goes through money as if there's no tomorrow. I've pampered and indulged her since Mary died, and now I'm left to deal with it."

"But she's such a dear child."

"Dear, but hopelessly unhappy, I fear. The thing is—" her father's voice lowered and took on a slightly husky quality "—I don't know how to help her."

A twinge of guilt caused Elizabeth to lower her head fractionally. She'd thought she had concealed her unhappiness. And she couldn't argue with her father's earlier statement. Her spending *had* been extravagant the last few months.

"What can we do?" Again, it was her grandmother.

"I don't know, Mother."

Elizabeth had never heard such resignation from her father. "I'll talk to her, but I don't know what good it will do. Perhaps if Mary had lived..." he continued soberly.

Elizabeth refused to listen to any more. Her father rarely spoke of her mother. Mary Elizabeth Wainwright's unexpected death two years before still had the power to inflict a deep sense of loss on them both. Elizabeth's brother had adjusted well, but he was older and constitutionally more able to cope with his grief.

Thoughtfully, she climbed the long, winding staircase to her rooms. A confrontation with her father was the last thing she wanted. How could she explain this lackadaisical attitude that had taken over her usually cheerful existence? And as for the benefits of wealth, she was well aware of the privileges and even the power that came with having money. But money wasn't everything; it didn't bring happiness or fulfillment. The best time she'd had in her life had been the summer she bummed her way across France, when she'd barely had two euros to rub together. Not only was she intelligent, she was gifted. She spoke fluent French, and enough Italian and German to make her last visits to Rome and Berlin worry-free. But what good was any of that to her now?

Sitting on her plush canopy bed, she forced her spine to straighten. She was a Wainwright. She was supposed to maintain her pride and independence at all times.

A gnawing ache churned her stomach.

She didn't want to talk to her father. She didn't want to explain the fiasco in Paris and her extravagant expenses. All she wanted was peace and quiet. The germ of an idea began to form in her mind. Her bags were still packed. She could swear Bently to silence and slip out just as quietly as she'd slipped in. San Francisco sounded appealing. Her mother had spent a carefree summer there when she was about Elizabeth's age. With a renewed sense of purpose, she headed out of her bedroom door and down the back stairs.

One

The ever-present odor of fresh fish and the tangy scent of saltwater followed Elizabeth as she sauntered down Fisherman's Wharf. The wharf wasn't far from where she was staying at the St. Francis, one of San Francisco's most prestigious hotels. A little breeze ruffled her golden-brown hair and added a shade of color to her otherwise pale features.

With the morning paper tucked under her arm, she strolled into a small French café. It had only taken three days for the restless boredom to make its way into her thoughts. How could she sit in one of the most beautiful cities in the world with the homey scent of freshly baked bread drifting from the restaurant kitchen and feel this listless?

A friendly waitress dressed in a crisp pink uniform with a starched white apron took her order for coffee and a croissant. She wasn't hungry, but she had noticed this morning that her clothes were beginning to hang on her and decided to make the effort to eat more.

Lackadaisically her eyes ran over the front page of the newspaper. Nothing had changed. The depressing stories of war and hate were the same on this day as they had been the week before and the month before that. Sighing, she folded the newspaper and waited for the waitress to bring her food.

"Are you looking for a job?" the young waitress asked eagerly as she delivered Elizabeth's order.

"I beg your pardon?"

"I saw you looking through the paper and thought you might be job-hunting. I wouldn't normally suggest something like this, but there's an opening here, if you'd like to apply. You could start right now."

Elizabeth's pale blue eyes widened incredulously. What was this girl talking about?

"I know it's not much, but a position here could tide you over until you find what you're really looking for. The other girl who normally works with me called in this morning and quit." She paused to forcefully release her breath. "Can you imagine? Without a minute's notice. Now I'm left to deal with the lunch crowd all by myself."

Elizabeth straightened in her chair. Why not? She didn't have anything better to do. "I don't know that I'd be much help. I've never been a waitress."

"It doesn't matter." The younger girl's relief was obvious. "I can guarantee that by the end of the day you'll discover everything you ever cared to know about waitressing and a few things you didn't." Her laugh was light and cheerful. "By the way, I'm Gilly. Short for Gillian."

"And I'm Elizabeth."

"Glad to meet you, Elizabeth. Boy, am I glad." The breezy laugh returned. "Come on back to the kitchen, and I'll introduce you to Evelyn. He's the owner and chef, and I'm *sure* he'll hire you." With determined, quick-paced steps, Gilly led the way across the room to the swinging double doors. She paused and turned around. "Don't be shocked if Evelyn kisses you or something. He's like that. I think it's because he's French."

"I won't be surprised," Elizabeth murmured and had trouble containing her smile. What would Gilly say if she knew that Elizabeth spoke the language fluently and had lived in Paris?

A variety of pleasant smells assaulted her as she entered the spotless kitchen. As a little girl, her favorite place in the huge, rambling house had been the kitchen. The old cook would often sneak her pieces of pie dough or a cookie. Her childhood had been happy and untroubled.

"Evelyn," Gilly said, attracting the attention of the chef who was garbed completely in white and working busily at the stove. "This is Elizabeth. She's going to take Deanne's place."

The ruddy-faced man with a thick mustache that was shaped like an open umbrella over a full mouth turned and stared blankly at Elizabeth.

Giving in to impulse, she took a step forward and extended her hand. In flawless French, she explained that she hadn't done any waitressing but would be pleased to help them out this afternoon.

Laughing, Evelyn broke into a wild speech in his native language while pumping her hand as if she were a long-lost relative.

Again in perfect French, she explained that no, she wasn't from France or Quebec, but she had spent several years studying in his country.

An expression of astonishment widened Gilly's eyes. "You should have said you were from France."

"I'm not. I studied French in school." Elizabeth didn't explain that the school had been in Paris.

"You know, that's one thing I'm sorry for," Gilly said, thoughtfully pinching her bottom lip. "I wish I'd studied French. A lot of good Spanish does me here. But then—" she paused and chuckled "—I could always end up working in a Mexican restaurant."

Elizabeth laughed. Gilly was delightful. Amiable and full of enthusiasm, the younger girl was just the antidote for the long day that lay ahead.

Luckily, the two were close enough in size that Elizabeth could wear one of Gilly's extra uniforms.

After a minimum of instruction, Elizabeth was given a pad and pencil, and asked to wait on her first customers, an elderly couple who asked for coffee and croissants. Without incident, Elizabeth delivered their order.

"This isn't so bad," she murmured under her breath to Gilly, who was busy writing out the luncheon specials on the chalkboard that would be displayed on the sidewalk.

"I took one look at you and knew you'd do great," Gilly stated cheerfully.

"You took one look at me and saw an easy mark." A smile revealed deep grooved dimples in each of Elizabeth's cheeks.

"Does everyone call you Elizabeth?" Briefly, Gilly returned her attention to the chalkboard. "You look more like a Beth to me."

Beth, Elizabeth mused thoughtfully. No one had called her that since her school days, and then only her best friends. After all, she was a Wainwright. "Elizabeth" was the dignified name her family preferred.

"Call me anything you like," she said in a teasing tone. "No, on second thought, you better stick with Beth."

A half-hour later Elizabeth was answering to a variety of names, among them "Miss" and "Waitress." Never had she imagined that such a simple job could be so demanding, or that there were so many things to remember. The easy acceptance given her by the customers was a pleasant surprise. Most of the café's luncheon crowd were regulars from office buildings close to the wharf. Several of them took the time to chat before ordering. A couple of men blatantly flirted with her, which did wonders for her sagging ego. A few asked about Deanne and weren't surprised when they learned that she'd quit.

The highlight of the afternoon came when she waited on a retired couple visiting from France. She spoke to them in their native language for so long that Gilly had to point out that there were several other customers who needed attention. Later Gilly was shocked to see that the couple had left a tip as large as the price of their meal.

"Tutor me in French, would you?" she joked, as she passed by carrying a glass coffeepot.

Elizabeth couldn't believe the time when she glanced at her gold wristwatch. Four o'clock. The day had sped past, and she felt exhilarated, better than she had in months. Tonight she wouldn't need a pill to help her sleep.

"You were terrific. Everyone was saying how great you were," Gilly said, laying on the praise. "A couple of regulars said they hope you'll stay. And even if it was your first time waitressing, you were as good as Deanne ever was."

After all the orders she had mixed up, Elizabeth was surprised Gilly thought so. Of course, she had eaten in some of the world's best restaurants and knew what kind of service to expect. But giving it was something else entirely.

"Would you consider staying on for a while?" Gilly's tone held a mixture of hope and doubt. "I'm sure this isn't the kind of job you want. But the pay isn't bad, and the tips are good."

Elizabeth hesitated. "I…I don't know."

"It would only be until we could find someone to replace you," Gilly added quickly. "That shouldn't be long. A week or two. Three months at the most."

"Three months?" Elizabeth gasped.

"Well, to be honest, Evelyn saw you with the French couple and told me that he'd really like to hire you permanently. I suppose it's too much to ask, with your qualifications."

What qualifications? Elizabeth mused. Oh, sure, she knew all the finer points of etiquette, but aside from her fluency in several languages, she'd never had any formal job training.

"Just think about it, okay?" Gilly urged.

Elizabeth agreed with a soft smile.

"You'll be back tomorrow?" The doe-like eyes implored, making it impossible to refuse.

Exhaling slowly, Elizabeth nodded. "Sure. Why not?"

Why not indeed? she mused later as she unlocked the door to her suite at the

St. Francis. Her feet hurt, and there was an ache in the small of her back, but otherwise she felt terrific.

The hot water filling the tub was steaming up the bathroom when she straightened, struck by a thought. There was no one she wanted to visit this summer, no place she wanted to go. There wasn't anything to stop her from working with Gilly. It would be fun. Well, maybe not fun, but…different, and she was definitely in the mood for different.

With the sound of the hot water still running behind her, she knotted the sash of her blue silk robe and eased her feet into matching slippers. Sitting atop the mattress, she reached for the phone. For the first time in months, she felt like talking to her father. He had a right to know where she was staying and what she was up to. Over the last year she'd given him enough to worry about.

Bently answered the phone. "Good

evening, Miss Elizabeth," he said after she identified herself.

"Hello, Bently. Is my father home?"

"I'll get him for you."

Had she detected a note of worry in Bently's tone? He was always so formal that it was difficult to discern any emotion.

"Elizabeth, dear." Her father spoke crisply. "Just exactly where are you?" He didn't wait for her to answer. "Bently said that you were home, and then, before anyone knew what had happened, you were off again."

"I'm sorry, Dad," she said, though in fact she wasn't the least bit regretful. "I'm in San Francisco. I've got a job."

"A job," her father repeated in a low, shocked tone. "Doing what?"

She laughed, mentally picturing the perplexed look working its way across her father's face. With a liberal arts degree as vague and unimpressive as her grades, she knew he doubted that anyone would want to hire her. "I'm a waitress in a small French café called The Patisserie."

"A waitress!" Charles Wainwright exploded.

"Now don't go all indignant on me. I know this is a shock. But I'm enjoying it. Some of the customers speak French, and the chef is from Paris."

"Yes, but…" Elizabeth could feel her father's shock. "But if you wanted to work," he went on, "there are a hundred positions more suited to you."

"Honestly, Dad, I'd think you'd be happy that I'm out of your hair for the summer. Wish me well and kiss Grandmother for me."

"Elizabeth…"

"My bath's running. I've got to go."

A resigned note she recognized all too well entered his voice. "Take care of yourself, my dear."

* * *

"This is working out great," Gilly commented at the end of Elizabeth's first week. "I don't know what it is, but there's something about you that the customers like."

"It's because I can pronounce the name of Evelyn's pastries," Elizabeth returned in a teasing voice.

"That's not it," Gilly contradicted with a slight quirk of her head. Her short, bouncy curls bobbed with the action. "Though having you speak French does add a certain class to the place."

"My French may be good, but my feet are killing me." She faked a small, pain-filled sigh and rubbed the bottom of one expensive loafer over the top of the other.

"Your feet wouldn't hurt if you were wearing the right shoes."

Elizabeth glanced at her Guccis and groaned. Heavens, she'd spent more on these leather loafers than she made in a week at this restaurant. How could they possibly be the wrong kind of shoe?

"If you like, we can go shopping after work and I'll show you what you should be wearing."

Gilly's offer was a pleasant surprise. "Yes, I'd like that."

"It'll give me an excuse not to go home." Discontent coated Gilly's normally happy voice.

"What's the matter with home?"

One petite shoulder rose in a half-hearted shrug. "Nothing, I guess. It's just that I turned twenty last month, and I hate living with my parents."

"So get an apartment." Elizabeth suggested the obvious, wondering why Gilly hadn't thought of that herself.

Gilly's returning smile was stiff. "So speaks the voice of inexperience. I don't suppose you've gone looking for apartments lately. Have you seen how high rent is these days?"

Elizabeth had continued to live at the St. Francis. The hotel was convenient, and what meals she didn't eat at the Patisserie were promptly delivered to her room after a simple phone call.

"It isn't that I haven't tried," Gilly continued. "I found a boarding house and stayed there until my mother found out about my neighbors."

"Your neighbors?"

"I admit they were a bit unusual," Gilly mumbled. "I never saw the girl in the room next to me, but every morning there were two empty yogurt cartons outside her door."

Elizabeth couldn't restrain her soft laugh. "Suspicious yogurt, huh?"

"That was nothing," Gilly continued, her own laugh blending with Elizabeth's. "The woman on the other side looked like a Russian weight lifter who had failed a hormone test. One look at her— or him, whichever the case may be—and my mother had me out of there so fast my head was spinning."

Elizabeth could sympathize with her friend. "I know what you mean. I moved away from home as soon as I could, too."

"And if I left, my younger sister could have her own room and…" Gilly paused, her hand gripping Elizabeth's forearm. "He's back."

"Who?" Elizabeth glanced up to see a tall, broad-shouldered man enter the café. The first thing that impressed her was his size. He was easily six foot four. Yet he carried himself with an unconscious grace that reminded her of a martial arts expert. He wasn't handsome. His jaw was too angular, too abrupt. His mouth was firm, and even from this distance she noticed that it was slightly compressed, as if something had displeased him.

"Him," Gilly whispered under her

breath. "How long has it been since you've seen such an indisputable stud?"

"Obviously too long," Elizabeth responded, picking up a menu and water glass. "But then, isn't one stud just like another?" she asked blandly. Although not strikingly handsome, this man was compelling enough to attract women's attention.

"One stud is just like another?" Gilly repeated on a low, disbelieving breath. "Beth, this guy is Secretariat."

Elizabeth had difficulty hiding her smile as she moved across to the room to deliver the ice water and menu.

Secretariat turned and watched her approach. Dark sunglasses reflected her silvery image and disguised his eyes. The glasses rested on a nose that could kindly be described as aquiline. He removed the glasses and set them on the table.

Not until she was at his table did she realize how big he actually was. Massive shoulders suited his height. His muscular biceps strained against a short-sleeved shirt stretched taut across a broad chest. She imagined that someone of his build would have difficulty finding clothes that were anything except tight. It was unfortunate that apparently he couldn't afford to have his clothes custom-made.

"Good afternoon," she said as she handed him the menu and set the glass on the red-checked tablecloth. Her heart lodged near her throat as his fingers innocently brushed hers. There was something indefinable about him that was almost intimidating. Not that he frightened her; "intrigued" was more the word.

"Hello." His smile revealed even white teeth. He opened the menu and quickly scanned it. Without looking at her he said, "Don't worry, I don't bite."

"I didn't think you did," she returned,

resenting his absolutely incorrect belief that she was easily intimidated.

"I'll have coffee. Nothing more." A scowl made its way across his face.

She wrote down his order, thinking that he didn't look like the type to indulge in delicate French pastries.

As she returned to the counter, she could feel his gaze leveled between her shoulder blades. She was accustomed to the admiring glances of men. She had what her grandmother referred to as the Wainwright coloring, a warm blend of colors that often generated curious stares. Her eyes were the palest blue and her hair a lush shade of golden brown, worn loose so that it curled in natural waves at her shoulders.

"Did you notice the muscles on him?" she muttered under her breath to Gilly as she laid a spoon to the saucer. "I bet this guy wrestles crocodiles for a living."

Gilly pretended to be wiping down the

long counter, her hand rubbing furiously as she stifled a giggle. "I think he's kinda cute."

"Yes, but you're so sweet you'd think boa constrictors were cuddly."

"He's different. I bet he's a real pussy-cat. Give me five minutes alone with him and I'll prove it."

"No way. He looks dangerous, like he would eat you for breakfast."

"You're teasing, aren't you?"

Elizabeth didn't answer as she delivered the coffee. Before she walked away, she noticed that he drank it quietly, cupping the mug with his massive hands as he stared out the window. A few minutes later, he stood and left a handful of change on the table, then turned to wink at Gilly.

"Goodbye." Gilly waved to him. "Come in again."

"I'd say you've got yourself an admirer," Elizabeth said, glancing from her friend to the retreating male figure.

"Not me," Gilly denied instantly. "He was watching you like a hawk. You're the one who interests him, not me."

"Then I give Tarzan to you," Elizabeth spoke somberly. "Men like him are a bit much for me." She had heard about egotistical males with bodies like his. They spent hours every day building up their muscles so they could stand in front of a mirror and admire themselves.

Just before closing time, Gilly stuck her head around the door into the kitchen, where Elizabeth was finishing refilling the condiments.

"I bet he works on the docks."

"Who?"

"Don't be obtuse."

"Oh, Tarzan. I suppose," Elizabeth murmured, not overly interested. "I don't think he'll be back."

"He will," Gilly asserted confidently.

"And sooner rather than later. There was a look in his eyes. He's attracted to you, Beth. Even I noticed." The implication was that Elizabeth should have recognized it, too.

Gilly was right. The next afternoon he arrived at the same time. Elizabeth was carrying a tray of dirty dishes to the counter when she brushed against his solid male figure.

"Excuse me." The low, almost gravelly tone left no doubt as to who was speaking.

"My fault," she muttered under her breath, disliking the uncomfortable warmth that emanated from the spot where their bodies had touched. Easily six inches taller than she was, Tarzan loomed above her. Most women would have been awed by his closeness. But the sensations she was feeling were more troubling for the way they intrigued her than frightening. He wasn't wearing his reflective glasses today. The color of his eyes, along with his guarded look, was a surprise. Their amber shade resembled burnished gold marked by darker flecks, and he was staring at her as intently as any jungle beast. Again she had the impression that this man could be dangerous. Gilly might view him as a gentle giant, but she herself wasn't nearly as confident.

"What did I tell you?" Gilly whispered in a know-it-all voice.

"I guess you know your ape-men," Elizabeth returned flippantly.

For a second Gilly looked stunned at Elizabeth's cynicism. "How can you look at someone as gorgeous as this guy and call him an ape?" Righteously, she tucked the menu under her arm. "I'm taking his order today," she announced, and she strolled across the floor.

Watching her friend's movements, Elizabeth had to stifle a small laugh. Gilly's walk couldn't be more obvious; she was interested in him, and before the afternoon was over, Tarzan would know it.

"His name's Andrew Breed," Gilly cheerfully informed her as she scooted past Elizabeth on her return. "But he says most everyone calls him Breed." She moved behind the counter before Elizabeth could respond.

Elizabeth was too busy with her own customers to notice much about either Gilly or Andrew Breed. Only once was she aware that he was studying her, his strong mouth quirked crookedly. His attention made her self-conscious. Once she thought he was going to ask her something, but if he was, the question went unasked. As he'd done the day before, he left the money for his coffee on the table and sauntered out of the café, this time before she was even aware he'd gone.

The remainder of the afternoon dragged

miserably. The weather was uncharacteristically hot and humid, and she could feel tiny beads of perspiration on her upper lip. A long soak in the bath, a light meal and the TV were sounding more appealing by the minute. She had spent most of her evenings looking for an apartment. The more she learned about Gilly's plight living at home, the more she wanted to help her friend. She had promised that if she found a place, they could move in together and share the rent, though Gilly need never know the actual figure.

Unfortunately, Elizabeth was quickly learning that Gilly hadn't underestimated the difficulty of finding a reasonably priced apartment in the city. She couldn't very well rent one for 2,000 a month and tell Gilly her share was 500. Her friend, although flighty, was smart enough to figure that out.

Gilly and Elizabeth worked together to close down the café that evening.

Elizabeth's thoughts were preoccupied as Gilly chattered away excitedly about one thing or another. The girl's boundless enthusiasm affected everyone she met. She was amazing.

In the small break room behind the kitchen, Elizabeth sat, kicked off her shoes and rubbed her aching feet. Gilly hobbled around, one shoe on and the other off as she opened her purse and dug around for something in the bottom of the large bag. "What's the big hurry?" Elizabeth inquired.

"What's the hurry?" Gilly stammered. "Breed'll be out front any minute. We're going to dinner."

"Breed?" Her heart did a tiny flip-flop. "You mean to say you're going out to dinner with someone you hardly know?"

"What do you think I was telling you?"

Elizabeth straightened and slipped her feet back into the new practical pumps she'd purchased with Gilly's approval. "I guess I wasn't paying any attention."

"I guess not!" Gilly shook her head and did a quick glance in the small mirror. "Oh dear, I'll never make it on time." Her delicate oval face creased with concern. "Beth, do me a favor. Go out front and tell him I'm running a little late. I'll be there in a few minutes."

"Sure." Her response was clipped and short. She didn't want to date Breed herself, but she wasn't sure how she felt about Gilly seeing him. The thought was so ridiculous that she pinched her mouth closed, irritated with herself.

"You don't mind, do you?" Gilly jerked her head around to study Elizabeth.

"Of course not. It's the least I can do to smooth the course of true love."

"Not about that," Gilly said.

Elizabeth tipped her head to one side in confusion.

"I mean about me going out with Breed."

"Me mind?" Elizabeth asked, giving an indifferent shrug. "Why should I care one way or the other?"

Gilly arched both nicely arched brows. "Because it's really you he's interested in."

"You keep saying that," Elizabeth said, shaking her head in denial. "Either you've got some sixth sense or I'm completely dense."

Without hesitation, Gilly threw back her head, her tight curls bouncing. "You're dense."

Resolutely squaring her shoulders, Elizabeth headed for the front of the café. Evelyn followed her out to lock the door after her, just as Gilly stuck her head around the kitchen door. "He's coming!" she cried. "I can see him across the street." Her round, panic-stricken eyes pleaded with Elizabeth. "Keep him occupied, will you?"

"Don't worry." She smiled at Evelyn on the other side of the glass door as he turned the lock. He looked at her and playfully rolled his eyes.

When Elizabeth turned around, she was only a few inches from Breed. This man had the strangest effect on her. She wasn't sure how she felt about him. His appeal blossomed with every encounter. It hadn't taken her long to realize that her first impression of him as a muscle-bound egomaniac was completely wrong. He seemed almost unaware of the effect he had on women.

"Gilly will be ready in a minute. She's changing clothes now."

The tight corners of Breed's mouth edged upward. "No problem. I'm early."

She folded her arms around her slim waist. "She's looking forward to tonight." Realizing her body language was revealing her state of mind, she quickly dropped her hands to her sides.

"I make you uncomfortable, don't I?"

Color rose from her neck, brightening her cheeks. "It's not that. I…I don't think I've ever known anyone quite like you."

"As big, you mean?"

"No, not that."

His strong, angular chin tilted downward fractionally. "And I don't think I've ever known anyone as beautiful as you." The words were soft, husky.

She sensed immediately that he wished he could withdraw them. He hadn't intended to say that. She was sure of it.

"My size *is* intimidating," he stated flatly, taking a step in retreat. There was a strong suggestion of impatience in the way he moved, something she hadn't noted in the past. And right now he was angry with himself.

Ignoring his strong, male profile, she

turned and looked up at the cloudless blue sky.

They both spoke at once.

"The weather…"

"How long…"

"You first." Breed smiled, and a pleasant warmth invaded her limbs.

"I was going to say that I was enjoying the weather this summer. After all that talk about the California smog and San Francisco's famous fog, I wasn't sure what to expect."

"You're not from California?" He looked surprised.

She didn't know why he should be; her light Boston accent wasn't difficult to decipher. "No, my roots are on the East Coast. Boston."

He nodded.

"Do you work on the wharf?" Conversation was easy with him; something else she hadn't expected. "Gilly and I were trying to guess."

"I'm a longshoreman."

It was her turn to give a polite nod. "It must be hard work." What else would give him muscles like that?

Fresh as a dewy rosebud, Gilly floated out the door in a light-blue summer dress. "Sorry to keep you waiting, Breed."

His amber eyes crinkled at the corners with a warm smile. "It was worth it," he said as he moved to her side, taking her hand in his.

Wiping a bead of perspiration from her forehead, Elizabeth gave Breed and Gilly a feeble smile. "Have fun, you two."

"Would you like to join us?" Gilly said.

Elizabeth took a step backward. As crazy as it sounded, she was half tempted. "I can't tonight. I'm going to look at another apartment."

"Beth, it's hopeless," Gilly said, her voice emphatic.

Breed's eyes surveyed her with open

interest. "You're looking for an apartment?"

"Are we ever!" Gilly proclaimed enthusiastically.

"Let me know what happens. I might be able to find something for you. My brother-in-law manages a building, and he told me he has a vacancy coming."

Gilly almost threw herself into his arms. "Really? Can we see it soon? Oh, Beth, what do you think?"

Elizabeth's smile wasn't nearly as enthusiastic. If Breed's brother-in-law showed them the apartment, he was sure to mention the rent, and Elizabeth knew Gilly couldn't afford much.

"Let me check out this ad tonight, and we can talk about it later."

A half-hour later Elizabeth was soaking in a hot tub filled with light-scented bubble bath. With the back of her head resting against the polished enamel, she closed her eyes, regretting that she hadn't gone with Breed and Gilly.

Two

"Oh, Beth!" Gilly exclaimed as she hurriedly stepped from room to room of the two-bedroom apartment in the marina district. "I can hardly believe how lucky you were to find this place. It's perfect."

Elizabeth was rather proud of it herself. The building was an older brick structure that had recently been renovated. She'd been fortunate to find it, even more fortunate to have convinced Gilly and Gilly's parents that the rent was cheaper for the first six months because there was still construction going on in the building. The perfection of the apartment made her deception easier. She could afford to pay three-quarters of the rent without Gilly ever being the wiser.

Polished wooden floors in the entryway led to a large carpeted living room that made liberal use of skylights.

"I still can't believe it," Gilly said as she turned slowly, her head tilted back to view the boundless blue sky through the polished glass ceiling. "I never dreamed you'd find something like this. Did you see that kitchen?" She returned her attention to Elizabeth. "Even my mother doesn't have such new appliances." With a deep sense of awe, she stepped into the kitchen and ran her hand along the marble counter. "I can't believe how well everything is working out for us." Pausing to glance at her wristwatch, she shook her head. "I've got one last load to bring over. I shouldn't be more than an hour."

"Don't worry. I'll hold down the fort," Elizabeth returned absently.

There were several things she wanted to do herself, including grocery shopping. She could fill the cupboards and Gilly would have no way of knowing how much she'd spent. When they divided the bill, Gilly wouldn't realize that she was only paying a fraction of the total. Elizabeth was enjoying the small duplicity. With a growing sense of excitement, she changed her clothes and started to make out an errand list. The Wainwrights were known for their contributions to charity, but this wasn't charity. She felt as though she owed Gilly something. If it hadn't been for Gilly, she was convinced she would still be trapped in the sluggish indifference that had dominated her life these past months. Her mother would have liked Gilly. Elizabeth pulled herself up straight. She hadn't thought about her mother in weeks. Even so, the memory remained sharp, with the power to inflict deep emotional pain. Just then the doorbell chimed. She couldn't imagine who it could be. Her step quickened as she walked to the door and opened it.

"Hello, Breed." Her hand tightened on the glass doorknob.

He handed her a large bouquet of flowers. "Welcome to the neighborhood," he said with a boyish grin.

"You live around here?" Her voice caught in her throat as she accepted the flowers. "Come in, please. I'm not being much of a hostess." She stepped back to allow him to enter and closed the door with her foot. "Gilly isn't here, but you're welcome to come in and tour the place if you like."

A smile glinted from his eyes as he followed her into the kitchen. "I'd like."

Deftly, she arranged the flowers and set them in the middle of the round kitchen table before leading the way through the apartment, glossing over the details.

"You're renting this for how much?"

Her heart dropped to her stomach. Gilly had apparently said something to Breed about their rent. She gave a light, breezy laugh, or what she hoped sounded light and breezy, and repeated what she'd told Gilly.

"Funny, I didn't notice any construction." He stood at the picture window.

"Of course you didn't." She continued the deception while keeping her gaze lowered. "Even carpenters go home in the evening." She was rescued from any further explanation by Gilly, who breathlessly barged through the door carrying a large box.

"Let me help." Immediately Breed took it from her and helped her carry in the remaining boxes.

When they'd finished, Gilly strolled

into the kitchen. "Breed offered to take us out to dinner. You'll come, won't you?"

Elizabeth's gaze flittered past her friend to Breed. She was uncomfortably aware of the unspoken questions he was sending her way.

"Not this time."

Gilly exhaled a heavy breath and pushed the curls away from her face in an exasperated movement. "But you will soon, right?" She glanced from Breed to Elizabeth.

"Another time," Elizabeth agreed, going back to her list.

"Promise?" Gilly prompted.

"Promise," Elizabeth returned, unsure why she felt the way she did. There was something about Breed that troubled her. Not his size, although he was right: that in itself *was* intimidating. His eyes often held a mischievous glint, as if he knew something she didn't. Not that he was laughing at her—far from it. There was understanding, compassion, and sometimes she thought she caught a glimmer of something close to sympathy. He was a complicated man, and she was afraid that if she investigated further, she would like him a lot more than she had a right to.

She should have realized that neither of them would go on accepting her refusal to join them. The following Saturday Gilly was adamant that Elizabeth go with them to the beach.

"You're coming!" she insisted, stuffing an extra beach towel in her bag.

"Gilly..." Elizabeth moaned.

"It's a gorgeous day. How can you even think about sitting at home when you can be lazing on the beach, soaking up the sun?"

"But I don't want to intrude."

"Intrude? Are you nuts? We want you to come."

Gilly had gone out with Breed twice

in the last week. They'd asked Elizabeth along both times.

Elizabeth liked Breed. The intensity of her feelings both surprised and alarmed her. Each time Gilly and Breed went out they returned early, and then the three of them sat in the living room and talked while drinking coffee. At every meeting, Elizabeth grew more aware of him. Gilly had reacted naturally to the magnetic appeal of the man, but it had taken Elizabeth longer to recognize his potency.

He was a wonderful conversationalist. His experiences were broad and seemingly unlimited. Several times she had to bite her tongue to keep from revealing too much of herself and her background in response. In some ways she felt there wasn't anything she couldn't share with him.

She didn't know what to make of Gilly's relationship with him. They seemed to enjoy one another's company and had formed an easy friendship. But Gilly was the world's friend. After she and Breed had spent an evening together, Elizabeth would study her roommate closely. Gilly didn't appear to be falling in love, and Elizabeth found that conclusion comforting. Not that she was such an expert on love. There had been several times when she had wondered whether she was in love, but then she'd decided that if she had to wonder, she wasn't.

"Put on your swimsuit!" Gilly shouted from the kitchen now. "And hurry. Breed'll be here in ten minutes."

"You're sure you want me along?" Elizabeth continued to waver.

Gilly turned around and rolled her eyes theatrically. "Yes! You really do have a problem with the obvious, don't you?"

Elizabeth changed into her silky turquoise bikini. On the beaches of the Riviera, the skimpy two-piece had been modest. Now, studying herself in the mirror, she felt naked and more than a little vulnerable.

Gilly gave a low wolf whistle. "Wow! That doesn't look like it came from Best Beach Bargains dot com."

"Is it okay? There's not much to it." Elizabeth's gaze was questioning.

"I know. It's gorgeous—*you're* gorgeous."

"I'm not sure I should wear it…. I've got a sundress that would serve just as well."

"Elizabeth," Gilly insisted, "wear the bikini." She bit into a carrot stick. "Honestly, sometimes I swear you're the most insecure person I've ever met." She took the carrot stick out of her mouth and held it in her fingers like a cigarette. "By the way, where *did* you get that suit? I've never seen anything like it."

Elizabeth hesitated, her mind whirling

in a thousand directions. "A little place…
I don't remember the name."

"Well, wherever it is you shop, they
sure have beautiful clothes."

"Thank you," Elizabeth mumbled as
she put on a white cover-up. Quickly
she changed the subject. "You're looking great yourself."

Gilly lowered her gaze to her rose-
colored one-piece with a deep-veed neck-
line and halter top. "This old rag?"

"You just got that last week."

"I know, but next to you, it might as
well be a rag."

"Gilly, that's not true, and you know
it."

"Yes, but look at you. You're perfect.
There isn't anything I wouldn't sacrifice
for long legs and a figure like yours."

Elizabeth was still laughing when
Breed arrived. He paused and gave Gilly
an appreciative glance. "I should have

suggested the beach sooner. You look fantastic."

She positively sparkled under his appraisal. "Wait until you see Elizabeth's suit. She's the one with the glorious body."

Breed didn't comment, but he exchanged a meaningful glance with Elizabeth that said more than words.

Admittedly, she wanted to impress him. Deep within herself she yearned for his eyes to reveal the approval he had given Gilly. To divert her mind from its disconcerting course, she tightened the sash of her cover-up and added suntan lotion to her beach bag.

"I'm ready if you are," she said to no one in particular. She continued to feel a little uneasy infringing on Gilly's time with Breed, but she was pleased to be spending the day in the sun. In past summers she had prided herself on a luxurious tan. Already it was the third week of June, and she looked as pale as eggwhite.

An hour later they had spread a blanket on a crowded beach at Santa Cruz, sharing the sand with a thousand other sun-worshippers. Breed sat with his knees bent as Gilly smoothed lotion into his broad shoulders.

Mesmerized, Elizabeth couldn't tear her eyes away. Gilly's fingers blended the tanning lotion with the thin sheen of perspiration that slicked his muscular back. She rubbed him with slow, firm strokes until Elizabeth's mouth went dry. The bronze skin rippled with the massaging movements, his flesh supple under Gilly's manipulations. Lean and hard, Breed was excitingly, sensuously, all male.

Elizabeth's breath caught in her throat as Breed turned his head and she felt his gaze. His eyes roamed her face, pausing on the fullness of her lips. They were filled with silent messages meant only for her. They were messages she couldn't decipher, afraid of their meaning. Her cheeks suffused with hot color, and she dragged her eyes from his.

"You probably should put on some lotion, too, Elizabeth," he commented. The slight huskiness of his voice was the only evidence that he was as affected as she by their brief exchange.

"He's right," Gilly agreed. "When I've finished here, I'll do you."

Elizabeth was amused at the look of disappointment he cast her. He'd planned to do it himself, and Gilly had easily thwarted him.

After Gilly's quick application of lotion to her back, Elizabeth slathered her face, arms and stomach, and lay down on her big beach blanket. A forearm over her eyes blocked out the piercing rays of the afternoon sun. Pretending to be asleep, she was only half listening as

Breed and Gilly chatted about one thing or another.

"Hey, look!" Gilly cried excitedly. "They've started a game of volleyball. You two want to play?"

"Not me," Elizabeth mumbled.

"You go ahead," Breed insisted.

A spray of sand hit Elizabeth's side as Gilly took off running. Judging by her enthusiasm, no doubt she was good at the game.

"Mind if I share the blanket with you?" Breed asked softly.

"Of course not." Despite her words, her mind was screaming for him to join Gilly at volleyball.

He stretched out beside her, so close their thighs touched. She tensed, her long nails biting into her palms. Her nerves had fired to life at the merest brush of his skin against hers. She attempted to scoot away, but granules of sand dug into her shoulder blade, and she realized she couldn't go any farther.

Never had she been more acutely aware of a man. Every sense was dominated by him. He smelled of spicy musk and fragrant tobacco. Did he smoke? She couldn't remember seeing him smoke. Either way, nothing had ever smelled more tantalizing.

Salty beads of perspiration dotted her upper lip, and she forced her mouth into a tight line. If he were to kiss her she would taste the salty flavor of his… She sat up abruptly, unable to endure any more of these twisted games her mind was playing.

"I think I'll take a swim," she announced breathlessly.

"Running away?" His gaze mocked her.

"Running?" she echoed innocently. "No way. I want to cool down."

"Good idea. I could use a cold water

break myself." With an agility she was sure was unusual in a man his size, he got quickly to his feet.

As he brushed the sand from the backs of his legs, she ran toward the ocean. With her long hair flying behind her, she laughed as she heard him shout for her to wait. The water was only a few feet away, and they hit the pounding surf together.

The spray of cold water that splashed against her thighs took Elizabeth's breath away, and she stopped abruptly. Shouldn't the ocean off the California coast be warmer than this?

Breed dived into an oncoming wave and surfaced several feet away. He turned and waited for her to join him.

Following his lead, she swam to him, keeping her head above water as her smooth, even strokes cut into the swelling ocean.

"What's the matter?" he called. "Afraid to get your hair wet?"

"I don't want to look like Jack Sparrow."

He laughed, and she couldn't remember hearing a more exciting sound.

"You should laugh more often."

"Me?" A frown darkened his eyes. "You're the one who needs a few lessons on having fun." He placed a hand at her waist. "Let's take this wave together."

Without being given an option, she was thrust into the oncoming wall of water. As they went under the giant surge, she panicked, frantically lashing out with her arms and legs.

Breed pulled her to the surface. "Are you all right?"

"No," she managed to say, coughing and choking on her words. Saltwater stung her eyes. Her hair fell in wet tendrils over her face. "You did that on purpose," she accused him angrily.

"Of course I did," he countered. "It's supposed to be fun."

"Fun?" she spat. "Marie Antoinette's walk to the guillotine was more fun than that."

Breed sobered. "Come on. I'll take you back to the blanket."

"I don't want to go back." Another wave hit her, and her body rolled with it, her face going below the surface just as it crested. Again she came up coughing.

He joined her and helped her find her footing. "This is too much for you."

"It isn't," she sputtered. "If this is supposed to be fun, then I'll do it." With both hands she pushed the wet, stringy hair from her face. The feel of his body touching hers was doing crazy things to her equilibrium. The whole world began to sway. It might have been the effect of the ocean, but she doubted it.

"Will you teach me, Breed?" she requested in a husky whisper. She felt his body tense as the movement of the Pacific tide brought him close.

"Hold on," he commanded, just as another wave engulfed them.

She slipped her arms around his neck and held her breath. His arms surrounded her protectively, pressing her into the shelter of his body. Their feet kicked in unison, and they broke the surface together.

"How was that?" he asked.

Her eyes still closed, she nodded. "Better." Why was she kidding herself? This was heaven. Being held by Breed was the most perfect experience she could remember. That took her by surprise. She'd been held more intimately by others.

Slowly she opened her eyes. He pushed the hair from her face. "You're slippery," he murmured, pulling her more tightly into his embrace. His massive hands found their place at the small of her back.

"So are you. It must be the suntan lotion." Her breasts brushed his torso, and shivers of tingling desire raced through her. Such a complete physical response was as pleasant as it was unexpected.

"Watch out!" he called as they took the next wave. With their bodies intertwined, they rode the swell together.

A crooked smile was slanting Breed's mouth as they surfaced. Again his fingers brushed the long strands of wet hair from her face. He tucked them behind her ear, exposing her neck.

Elizabeth could feel the pulse near her throat flutter wildly. He pressed his fingertips to it and raised his eyes to her. In their golden depths she read desire, regret, surprise. He seemed to be as unprepared for this physical attraction as she was.

His mouth gently explored the pounding pulse in her neck. Moaning softly, she rolled her head to one side. His lips teased her skin, sending unanticipated shivers of delight washing over her. When he stopped, his eyes again sought hers.

"You taste salty."

Words refused to form. It was all she could do to nod.

He had come with Gilly. She had no right to be in the ocean with him, wanting him to kiss her so badly that she could feel it in every pore of her body.

"We should go back." She heard the husky throb in her voice.

"Yes," he agreed.

But they didn't move.

His crooked grin returned. "Did you have fun?"

She nodded.

"I'm sorry about your hair."

"Are you trying to tell me I look like Jack Sparrow?"

"No. If you want the truth, I've never seen you look more beautiful."

Her skin chilled, then flushed with

warmth. She couldn't believe that his words had the power to affect her body temperature.

"You're being too kind," she murmured, the soft catch in her voice revealing the effect of his words.

They lingered in the water as if they both wanted to delay the return to reality for as long as possible. Then, together, they walked out of the surf, hand in hand.

When they reached their blanket, he retrieved their towels. "Here." He handed her the thickest one and buried his face in his own.

Sitting on the blanket, Elizabeth dug through her beach bag and came up with a comb. She was running it through her hair when Gilly came rushing up, a tall, blond man beside her.

"Breed and Elizabeth, this is Peter."

"Hi, Peter." Breed rose to his feet, standing several inches taller than the other man. The two of them shook hands. For a second Breed looked from Gilly to Peter, then back again. His brows pulled into a thick frown.

"Peter invited me to stay and play volleyball, then grab some dinner," Gilly explained enthusiastically. "He said he'd take me home later. You two don't mind, do you?"

Elizabeth's eyes widened with shock. Did Gilly honestly believe she should come to the beach with one man and leave with another?

"We don't mind," Breed answered for them both.

"You're sure?" Gilly seemed to want Elizabeth's approval.

"Go ahead," Elizabeth murmured, but her eyes refused to meet Gilly's.

"You guys looked like you were having fun in the water."

A gust of wind whipped Elizabeth's wet hair across her face. She pushed it aside. The action gave her vital moments to compose herself. Obviously Gilly had been watching her. Worse, it could be the reason her roommate had decided to stay there with Peter. She couldn't allow that to happen.

"We had a wonderful time." Breed answered for them both again.

"I'll see you tonight, then," Gilly said, walking backward as she spoke.

Frustrated, Elizabeth called out for Gilly to wait, but her friend ignored her, turned, and took off running. "We can't let her do that," she told Breed.

"What?" A speculative light entered his eyes.

"What's the matter with the two of you? Gilly's going off with a complete stranger. It isn't safe." She tugged the comb through her hair angrily. "Heaven knows what she's walking into. You didn't have to be so willing to agree to her crazy schemes. I'm not going to leave this beach without her." She knew she should say something about her fear that her own behavior with him had led to Gilly's decision, but her courage failed her.

"She's twenty and old enough to take care of herself." Despite his words, his low voice contained a note of vague concern.

"She's too trusting."

Ignoring her, he opened the cooler he'd brought and took out a bucket of chicken. "Want a piece?" he questioned, biting into a leg.

"Breed..." Elizabeth was quickly losing her patience. They were an hour from San Francisco, and he was literally handing Gilly over to a stranger.

"All right." He expelled his breath forcefully and closed the lid on the food. "Gilly knows Peter. I introduced them last week."

"What?" she gasped. None of this was making sense.

"The last time I went out with Gilly, we were really meeting Peter."

"I don't believe this."

"I didn't exactly need an expert to see that it was going to take weeks of coming to the Patisserie before you'd agree to go out with me."

"What's that got to do with anything?"

"Plenty." He didn't sound thrilled to be revealing his motivations. "I don't blame you. I know I can be a little intimidating at first."

She wanted to explain that it wasn't his size that intimidated her, but she didn't know how to account for her reticence. She couldn't very well explain that it was the way his eyes looked in a certain light or something equally vague. "So you dated Gilly instead?"

He nodded. "She knew that first night it was you I was interested in.

We planned this today." The tone of his voice relayed his unwillingness to play the game.

No wonder Gilly had been so anxious for her to join them every time she'd gone out with Breed.

"But you looked surprised when Gilly brought Peter over." She recalled the partially concealed question his eyes had shot at Gilly and Peter.

"Those two should be nominated for the Academy Award. They were supposed to have been long-lost friends." His jaw tightened as he turned away from her to look out over the ocean. His profile was strong and masculine.

"You didn't have to tell me." His honesty was a measure of how much he cared.

"No, I didn't. But I felt you had the right to know." His arms circled his bent knees. "I hope Gilly realizes what a good friend you are."

Lightly, she traced her fingers over the corded muscles of his back. A smile danced at the edges of her mouth as she stretched out on the blanket. "No, I think you've got the facts wrong. It's me who needs to thank Gilly."

He turned just enough so that he could see her lying there, looking up at him.

"How could I have been so stupid?" She whispered the question, staring into the powerful face of this man whose heart was just as big as the rest of him.

He lay on his stomach beside her.

"Have you always been big?"

"Have you always had freckles on your nose?" he asked, turning the tables on her. His index finger brushed the tip of her nose.

Her hand flew to her face. "They're ugly. I've hated them all my life."

"You disguise them rather well."

"Of course I do. What woman wants orange dots glowing from her nose?"

"They're perfect."

"Breed," she said, raising herself up so that she rested her weight on her elbows, "how can you say that?"

"Maybe it's because I find you to be surprisingly delightful. You're refreshingly honest, hard-working, and breathtakingly beautiful."

She recalled all the flattery she'd received from men who had something to gain by paying attention to her. A large inheritance was coming to her someday. That was enough incentive to make her overwhelmingly attractive to any man.

But here she was on a crowded California beach with someone who didn't know her from Eve. And he sincerely found her beautiful. She cast her gaze downward, suddenly finding her deception distasteful. A lone tear found its way to the corner of her eye.

"Elizabeth, what's wrong?"

She didn't know how she could explain. "Nothing," she returned softly. "The wind must have blown sand in my eye." By tilting her chin upward toward the brilliant blue sky, she was able to quell any further emotion.

She lay down again, resuming her sun-soaking position. Breed rolled over, positioning himself so close she felt his skin brush hers.

"Comfortable?" he asked.

"Yes."

His large hand reached for hers, and they just lay there together, fingers entwined. They didn't speak, but the communication between them was stronger than words.

Finally she dozed.

"Elizabeth." A hand at her shoulder shook her lightly. "If you don't put something on, you'll get burned."

Struggling to a sitting position, she discovered Breed kneeling above her, holding out her cover-up. "You'd better wear this."

She put it on. "Is there any of that chicken left?"

"Are you hungry?"

"Starved. I was in such a rush this morning, I didn't eat breakfast."

Opening the cooler, Breed fixed her a plate of food that was enough to feed her for three meals.

She didn't say so, though. She just took a big bite of the chicken. Fabulous. But she couldn't decide if it was the meal or the man.

The sun had sunk into a pink sky when Breed pulled up to the curb outside her apartment.

"You'll come in for coffee, won't you?" Elizabeth spoke the words even though they both knew that coffee had nothing to do with why he was coming inside.

She continued with the pretense, filling the coffeemaker with water and turning it on. She turned to discover his smoldering amber eyes burning into her. Her heart skipped a beat, then accelerated wildly at the promise she read there.

Wordlessly, she walked into his arms. This was the first time he'd held her outside the water, and she was amazed at how perfectly their bodies fitted together. The top of her head was tucked neatly under his chin.

Her smile was provocative as she slipped her arms around his neck and tilted her head back to look up at him.

His eyes were smiling back at her.

"What's so amusing?"

"The glow from your freckles is blinding me."

"If I wasn't so eager for you to kiss me, I'd make you pay for that remark."

Breed lowered his mouth to an inch above hers. "I have a feeling I'm going to pay anyway," he murmured as he tightly wrapped his arms around her.

Being so close to this vibrant man was enough to disturb her senses. She tried to ignore the myriad sensations his touch aroused in her. As silly and crazy as it seemed, she felt like Sleeping Beauty waiting for the kiss that would awaken her after a hundred years.

Tenderly his mouth brushed over her eyelid, causing her lashes to flutter shut. Next he kissed her nose. "I love those freckles," he whispered.

Lastly he kissed her mouth with a masterful possession that was everything she had dreamed a kiss could be. It was a kiss worth waiting a hundred years for. He was gentle yet possessive. Pliant yet hard. Responsive yet restrained.

"Oh, Breed," she whispered achingly.

"I know." He breathed against her temple. "I wasn't expecting this, either."

She closed her eyes and breathed in

the mingled scent of spicy musk and saltwater. With her head pressed close to his heart, she could hear the uneven beat and knew he was as overwhelmed as she was at how right everything felt between them.

"I should go," he mumbled into her hair. He didn't need to add that he meant he should leave while he still had the power to pull himself out of her arms. "Can I see you tomorrow?"

Eagerly, she nodded.

He pulled away. "Walk me to the door."

She did as he requested. He kissed her again, but not with the intensity of the first time. Then, lightly, he ran one finger over her cheek. "Tomorrow," he whispered.

"Tomorrow," she repeated, closing the door after him.

Three

Elizabeth adjusted the strap of her pink linen summer dress as Gilly strolled down the hall and leaned against the doorjamb, studying her. "Hey, you look fantastic."

"Thanks." Elizabeth's smile was uneasy. Breed had been on her mind all day, dominating her thoughts, filling her consciousness. Yesterday at the beach could have been a fluke, the result of too much sun and the attention of an attractive man. Yet she couldn't remember a day she had enjoyed more. Certainly not in the last two years. Breed made her feel alive again. This morning she'd been cooking her breakfast and humming. She couldn't remember the last time she'd felt so content. When she was with him, she wanted to laugh and throw caution to the wind.

Continuing to date him was doing exactly that. She couldn't see herself staying in San Francisco past the summer. When it came time to return to Boston, her heart could be so entangled with Breed that leaving would be intolerable. No, she decided, she had to protect herself...*and* him. He didn't know who she was, and she could end up hurting him. She couldn't allow herself to fall in love with him. She had to guard herself against whatever potential there was to this relationship. She couldn't allow this attraction to develop into anything more than a light flirtation.

"I sure wish I knew where you got

your clothes," Gilly continued to chatter. "They're fantastic."

Elizabeth ignored the comment. "Do you think I'll need the jacket?" The matching pink top was casually draped over her index finger as her gaze sought Gilly's.

Gilly gave a careless shrug, crossing her arms and legs as she gave Elizabeth a thorough inspection. "I think I'd probably take it. You can never be certain what the weather's going to do. Besides, Breed may keep you out into the early-morning hours."

"Not when I have to work tomorrow, he won't," Elizabeth returned confidently.

The doorbell chimed just as she finished rolling the lip gloss across the fullness of her bottom lip.

"I'll get it," Gilly called from the kitchen.

Placing her hands against the dresser

to steady herself, Elizabeth inhaled, deeply and soothingly, and commanded her pounding heart to be still. The way she reacted to Breed, someone would think she was a sixteen-year-old who had just been asked out by the captain of the football team.

"It's Breed," Gilly said, sauntering into the room.

Elizabeth gave herself one final inspection in the dresser mirror. "I thought it must be." Folding her jacket over her forearm, she walked into the living room, where he was waiting.

"Hi," she said as casually as possible. He looked good. So good. His earthy sensuality was even more evident now than in the dreams her mind had conjured up the previous night. Suddenly she felt tongue-tied and frightened. She could so easily come to love this man.

"Beth didn't say where the two of you

were going," Gilly said before biting into a crisp apple.

"I thought we'd take in the outdoor concert at the Sigmund Stern Grove. A cabaret sextet I'm familiar with is scheduled for this afternoon. That is—" he hesitated and caught Elizabeth's eye "—unless you have any objection."

"That sounds great." By some miracle she found her voice. The corded muscles of Breed's massive shoulders relaxed. If she hadn't known better she would have guessed that he was as nervous about this date as she was. He glanced at his watch. "If we plan to get a seat in the stands, then I suggest we leave now."

Gilly followed them to the door. "I won't wait up for you," she whispered, just loud enough for Elizabeth to hear.

"I won't be late," Elizabeth countered with a saccharine-sweet smile, discounting her friend's assumption that she wouldn't be home until the wee hours of the morning.

Breed opened the door to a late-model, mud-splattered, army-green military-style Jeep and glanced up at her quizzically. "I had to bring Hilda today. Do you mind?"

A Jeep! The urge to laugh was so strong that she had to hold her breath. She'd never ridden in one in her life. "Sure, it looks like fun."

His hand supported the underside of her elbow as she climbed inside the vehicle. A vague disturbance fluttered along her nerve-endings at his touch, as impersonal as it was. He'd placed a blanket over the seat to protect her dress. His thoughtfulness touched her heart. The problem was, almost everything about this man touched her heart.

Once she was seated inside the open Jeep, her eyes were level with his. She turned and smiled as some of the nervous tension flowed from her.

When his warm, possessive mouth claimed her lips, Elizabeth's senses were overwhelmed with a rush of pleasure. The kiss, although brief, was ardent, and left her weak and shaking. Abruptly, Breed stepped back, as though he had surprised himself as much as he did her.

Dazed, she blinked at him. "What was that for?" she asked breathlessly.

He walked around to the other side of the Jeep and climbed inside without effort. He gripped the steering wheel as he turned and grinned at her. "For being such a good sport. To be honest, I thought you'd object to Hilda."

"To a fine lady like Hilda?" she teased. A trace of color returned to her bloodless cheeks. "Never. Why do you call her Hilda?"

"I don't know." He lifted one shoulder in a half-shrug. "Her personality's a lot like a woman's. It seems when I least expect trouble, that's when she decides to break down." The mocking glint of laughter touched his amber eyes. "She's as temperamental as they come."

"Proud, too," Elizabeth commented, but her words were drowned out by the roar of the engine. Hilda coughed, sputtered, and then came to life with a vengeance.

"See what I mean?" he said as he shifted gears and pulled onto the street.

By the time they'd reached the park, her carefully styled hair was a mess. The wind had whipped it from its loose chignon and carelessly tossed it about her neck and face.

"You all right?" he asked with a mischievous look in his eye.

She opened her purse and took out a brush. "Just give me a minute to comb my hair and scrape the bugs from my teeth and I'll be fine."

The pleasant sound of his laughter caused the sensitive muscles of her flat stomach to tighten. "I think Hilda must like you," he said as he climbed out and slammed the door. "I know I do." The words were issued under his breath, as if he hadn't meant for her to hear them.

The park was crowded, the free concerts obviously a popular program of the Parks and Recreation Department. Already the stands looked full, and it didn't seem as if they would find seats together. Other couples had spread blankets on the lush green grass.

With a guiding hand at her elbow, he led her toward the far end of the stands. "I think we might find a seat for you over here."

"Breed." She stopped him and turned slightly. "Couldn't we take the blanket from Hilda and sit on the lawn?"

"You'd want to do that?" He looked shocked.

"Why not?"

His eyes surveyed her dress, lingering momentarily on the jutting swell of her breasts. "But you might ruin your dress."

A flush of heat warmed her face at the bold look he was giving her. "Let me worry about that," she murmured, her voice only slightly affected.

"If you're sure." His eyes sought hers.

"Get the blanket, and I'll find us a place to sit."

A few minutes later they settled onto the grass and waited silently for the music to start. She had sat in the great musical halls of Europe and throughout the United States, but rarely had she anticipated a concert more. When the first melodious strains of a violin echoed through the air, she relaxed and closed her eyes.

The sextet proved to be as versatile as they were talented. The opening selection was a medley of classical numbers that she recognized and loved. Enthusiastic applause showed the audience's approval. Then the leader came to the front and introduced the next numbers, a variety of musical scores from classic films.

She shifted position, the hard ground causing her to fold her legs one way and then another.

"Here," Breed whispered, situating himself so that he was directly behind her, his legs to one side. "Use me for support." His hands ran down her bare arms as he eased her body against his. After a while she didn't know which score was louder, the one the musicians were playing or the one in her heart.

After the hour-long concert, Breed took her to a restaurant that he claimed served the best Mexican food this side of the Rio Grande.

"What did you think?" he asked as they sat across from one another in the open-air restaurant, eating cheese enchiladas and refried beans.

A gentle breeze ruffled her sandy hair about her shoulders as she set her fork aside. "How do I feel about the concert or the food?"

"The concert." He pushed his plate aside, already finished, while she was only half done.

"It was great. The whole afternoon's been wonderful." She cupped a tall glass of iced tea. Breed would be taking her home soon, and already she was dreading it. This day had been more enjoyable than all of the last six months put together, and she didn't want it to end. Every minute they were together was better than the one before. It sounded silly, but she didn't know how else to describe her feelings. Deliberately she took a long sip of her drink and set her fork aside.

"Are you finished already?"

Her gaze skimmed her half-full plate, and she nodded, her appetite gone.

"I suppose we should think about getting you back to the apartment."

Her heart sang at the reluctance in his voice. For one perfect moment their gazes met and locked. She didn't want to go home, and he didn't want to take her.

"How about a walk along the beach?" he suggested with a hint of reluctance.

She wondered why he was wary. Afraid of what she made him feel? No matter. She herself demonstrated no such hesitation. "Yes, I'd like that."

Hilda delivered them safely to an ocean beach about fifteen minutes outside the city. Others apparently had the same idea; several couples were strolling the sand, their arms wrapped around one another's waists.

"Do you need to scrape the bugs from your teeth this time?" Breed asked as he shifted into Park and turned off the engine. A smile was lurking at the edges of his sensuous mouth.

"No," she replied softly. "I've discovered that the secret of riding in Hilda is simply to keep my mouth closed."

His answering smile only served to remind her of the strength and raw virility that were so much a part of him. Her gaze rested admiringly on the smoothly hewn angles of his face as he climbed out of the Jeep and came around to her side. She must have been crazy to ever have thought of him as an ape-man. The thought produced a grimace of anger at herself.

"Is something wrong?" He even seemed sensitive to her thoughts.

"It's nothing," she said, dismissing the question without meeting his gaze.

Again his touch was impersonal as he guided her down a semi-steep embankment. A small, swiftly flowing creek separated them from the main part of the beach.

She hesitated as she searched for the best place to cross.

"What's the matter?" he teased with a vaguely challenging lilt to his voice. "Are you afraid of getting your feet wet?"

"Of course not," she denied instantly. "Well, maybe a little," she amended with a sheepish smile. It wasn't the water as much as the uncertainty of how deep it was.

"Allow me," he said as he swept her into his arms. One arm supported her back and the other her knees. Her hands flew automatically to his neck.

"Breed," she said under her breath, "what are you doing?"

"What any gallant gentleman would do for a lady in distress. I'm escorting you to safety." His amber eyes were dancing with mischief. He took a few steps and teetered, causing her grip on his neck to tighten.

"Breed!" she cried. "I'm too heavy. Put me down."

His chiseled mouth quirked teasingly as he took a few more hurried steps and delivered her safely to the other side. When he set her down, she noticed that his pants legs were soaking wet.

"You *are* a gallant knight, aren't you." Her inflection made the question a statement of fact.

Something so brief that she thought she'd imagined it flickered in his expression. It came and went so quickly she couldn't decipher its meaning, if there was one.

The dry sand immediately filled her sandals, and after only a few steps she paused to take them off. He did the same, removing his shoes and socks, and setting them beside a large rock. She tossed hers to join his.

They didn't say anything for a long time as they strolled, their hands linked. He positioned himself so that he took the brunt of the strong breeze that came off the water.

Elizabeth had no idea how far they'd gone. The sky was a glorious shade of pink. The blinding rays of the sinking sun cast their golden shine over them as they continued to stroll. The sight of the lowering sun brought a breathless sigh of wonder from her lips as they paused to watch it sink beneath the horizon.

Watching the sun set had seemed like such a little thing, and not until this moment, with this man at her side, had she realized how gloriously wondrous it was.

"Would you like to rest for a while before we head back?" he suggested. She agreed with a nod, and he cleared her a space in the dry sand.

With her arms cradling her knees, she looked into a sky that wasn't yet dark.

"How long will it be before the stars come out?"

"Not long," Breed answered in a low whisper, as if he were afraid words would diminish the wonder of the evening. Leaning back, he rested his weight on the palms of his hands as he looked toward the pounding waves of the ocean. "What made you decide to come to San Francisco?" he asked unexpectedly.

Elizabeth felt her long hair dance against the back of her neck in the breeze. "My mother. She spent time here the summer before she married my father, and she loved it." Her sideward glance encountered deep, questioning eyes. "Is something wrong?"

He was still. "Are you planning on getting married?"

She wasn't sure she was comfortable with this line of questioning. "Yes," she answered honestly.

He sat up, and she noticed that his

mouth had twisted wryly. "I wish you'd said something before now." The steel edge of his voice couldn't be disguised.

"Well, doesn't everyone?"

"Doesn't everyone what?" His fragile control of his temper was clearly stretched taut.

Scooting closer to his side, she pressed her head against his shoulder. "Doesn't everyone think about getting married someday?"

"So is there a Mr. Boston Baked Bean sitting at home waiting for you?"

"Mr. Boston Baked Bean?" She broke into delighted peals of laughter. "Honestly, Breed, there's no one."

"Good." He groaned as he turned and pressed her back against the sand. Her startled cry of protest was smothered by his plundering mouth. Immediately her arms circled his neck as his lips rocked over hers in an exchange of kisses that stirred her to the core of her soul.

Restlessly his hands roamed her spine as he half lifted her from the soft cushion of the sandy beach. She arched against him as he sensually attacked her lower lip, teasing her with biting kisses that promised ecstasy but didn't relieve the building need she felt for him.

"Breed," she moaned as her hands cupped his face, directing his hungry mouth to hers. Anything to satisfy this ache inside her. A deep groan slipped from his throat as she outlined his lips with the tip of her tongue.

Breed tightened his hold, and his mouth feasted on hers. He couldn't seem to give enough or take enough as he relaxed his grip and pressed her into the sand. Desire ran through her bloodstream, spreading a demanding fire as he explored the sensitive cord of her neck and paused at the scented hollow of her throat.

Her nails dug into his back as she shuddered with longing.

She felt the roughness of his calloused hand as he brushed the hair from her face. "I shouldn't have done that," he whispered. His voice was filled with regret. With a heavy sigh, he eased his weight from her. "Did I hurt you?" He helped her into a sitting position, but his hand remained on the curve of her shoulder, as if he couldn't let go.

"You wouldn't hurt me," she answered in a voice so weak she felt she had to repeat the point. "I'm not the least bit hurt." Lovingly, her finger traced the tight line of his jaw. "What's wrong? You look like you're sorry."

He nestled her into his embrace, holding her as he had at the concert, his arms wrapped around her from behind. His chin brushed against the crown of her head.

"Are you sorry?" She made it a question this time.

"No," he answered after a long time, his voice a whisper, and she wondered if he was telling the truth.

Without either of them being aware of it, darkness had descended around them. "The stars are out," she commented, disliking the finely strung tension their silence produced. "When I was younger I used to lean out my bedroom window and try to count the stars."

"I suppose that was a good excuse to stay up late," he said, his voice thick, rubbing his chin against her hair.

She smiled to herself but didn't comment.

His embrace slackened. "Do you want to go?"

"No." Her response was immediate. "Not yet," she added, her voice losing some of its intensity. She shifted position so that she lay back, her head supported by his lap as she gazed into the brilliant heavens. "It really is a gorgeous night."

"Gorgeous," he repeated, but she noted he was looking down on her when he spoke. "You certainly have a way of going to my head, woman."

"Do I?" She sprang to a sitting position. "Oh, Breed, do I really?"

He took her hand and placed it over his pounding heart. "That should answer you."

She let her hands slide over his chest and around his neck. Twisting, she turned and playfully kissed him.

"But the question remains, do I do the same thing to you?" he asked, his voice only slightly husky.

Elizabeth paused and shifted until she was kneeling at his side. Their eyes met in the gilded glow of the moon. "What does this tell you?" she said, more serious than she had been in her life. Taking his hand, she pressed it against her heart, holding it there as he inhaled a quivering breath.

"It tells me—" he hesitated as if gathering his resolve "—that it's time to go." He surged to his feet, then offered her a hand to help her up.

With a smile, she slipped her fingers into his.

The walk back to the Jeep seemed to take forever. Surely they hadn't gone this far.

"Isn't that Hilda?" she asked, pointing to the highway up ahead.

"Couldn't be." He squinted against the dark. "We haven't gone far enough yet."

"Far enough?" she repeated incredulously. "We couldn't possibly have wandered much farther than this." Their portion of the beach was deserted now, although she noted a few small fires in the distance, proof that there were others around. "Isn't that the rock where we left our shoes?" She pointed at the large boulder directly ahead of them.

"No." He was adamant. "We have at least another half mile to go."

Another half mile? Elizabeth's mind shouted. Already a chill had rushed over her bare arms, and the sand squishing between her toes was decidedly wet. The surf was coming in, driving them farther and farther up the beach.

"I'm sure you're wrong," she told him with more confidence than she was feeling. "That's got to be the rock." She was unable to banish the slight quiver from her voice.

Angrily, he stripped off his shirt and placed it around her bare shoulders. "You're freezing." He made it sound like an accusation. "For heaven's sake, why didn't you say something?"

"Because I knew you'd do something silly like take off your shirt and give it to me," she shot back testily. "That's the rock, I'm sure of it," she reiterated, hurrying ahead. The only light was from the half moon above, and when she knelt down and discovered a sock, she leapt triumphantly to her feet. "Ah, ha!" She dangled it in front of his nose. "What did I tell you!"

"That's not mine," he returned impatiently. "Good grief, Elizabeth, look at the size. That belongs to a child."

"This is the rock," she insisted. "It's got to be."

"Fine." His voice was decidedly amused. "If this is the rock, then our shoes would be here. Right?" He crossed his arms and stared at her with amused tolerance.

Boldly, she met his glare. "Someone could have taken them," she stated evenly, feeling suddenly righteous.

"Elizabeth." He paused and inhaled a calming breath. "Trust me. The rock and Hilda are about a half-mile up the beach.

If you'll quit arguing with me and walk a little way, you'll see that I know what I'm talking about."

"No." She knotted her fists at her sides in angry resolve. "I'm tired and I'm cold, and I think you've entirely lost your sense of direction. If you feel this isn't the rock, then go ahead and go. I'll be waiting for you here."

"You're not staying alone."

"I'm not going with you."

His eyes became hard points of steel, then softened. "Come on, it's not far."

"No." She stamped her foot, and splashed grit and sand against her bare leg from an incoming wave.

"You're not staying."

"Breed, listen to reason," she pleaded.

A wave crashed against his leg and he shook his head grimly.

"All right," she suggested. "Let's make a wager. Are you game?"

"Why shouldn't I be? You're wrong."

The mood lightened immediately. "What do you want to bet?"

"I'll march the unnecessary half-mile up the beach with you. But once you realize you're wrong, you have to carry me piggyback on the return trip. Agreed?"

"Just a minute here." A smile twitched at the corners of his mouth. "What do I get if I'm right?"

"A personal apology?" she suggested, confident she wouldn't need to make one.

His look was thoughtful. "Not good enough."

She slowly moistened her lips and gently swayed her hips. "Ten slow kisses in the moonlight."

He shook his head. "That's *too* good."

She laughed. "Are you always so hard to please?"

"No," he grumbled. "Come on, we can figure it out as we walk." He draped his arm over her shoulders, pulling her close. She wasn't sure if it was because he was as cold as she was now or if he simply wanted her near his side. She tucked her arm around his waist, enjoying the cool feel of his skin against her.

"It's a good thing you've got those freckles," he said seriously about five minutes later. "Without those lighting the way, we'd be lost for sure."

In spite of herself, she laughed. Breed had the ability to do that to her. If someone else had made a similar comment she would have been angry and hurt. But not when it was Breed.

Ten minutes later they spied another large boulder in the distance.

"What did I tell you?" He oozed confidence.

"Don't be so sure of yourself," she returned, only slightly unnerved.

"If my eyes serve me right, someone was kind enough to place our shoes on top so they wouldn't be swept out with the waves."

Her confidence cracked.

"Listen, Sacajawea. If you ever get lost, promise me you'll stay in one place."

"I get the message," she grumbled.

"Promise me," he said more forcefully. "I swear, you'd argue with Saint Peter."

"Well, you're no saint," she shot back.

His grip tightened as his eyes looked into hers. "Don't remind me," he murmured just before claiming her lips in a hungry kiss that left her weak and breathless. "I think we'll go with those ten kisses after all," he mumbled against her hair. "You still owe me nine."

By the time they made it up to the highway and Hilda, then found an all-night restaurant and had coffee, it was well after one. And it was close to two when Elizabeth peeled back the covers to her bed.

When the alarm went off a few hours later, she was sure the time was wrong.

Her eyes burned, and she felt as if she'd hardly slept.

Gilly was up and dressed by the time Elizabeth staggered into the kitchen and poured herself a cup of strong coffee.

"What time did you get in?" Gilly asked cheerfully.

"Two," Elizabeth mumbled almost inaudibly.

"I thought you were the one who insisted it was going to be an early night," Gilly said in a teasing, know-it-all voice.

"Do you have to be so happy in the morning?" Elizabeth grumbled, taking her first sip of coffee, nearly scalding her mouth.

"When are you seeing Breed again?"

He hadn't said anything the night before about another date. But they *would* be seeing one another again; Elizabeth had never been more sure of anything. A smile flitted across her face at the memory of their heated discussion about the rock. She could feel Gilly's gaze skimming over her.

"Obviously you're seeing him soon," the younger woman announced, heading toward her bedroom.

Breed came into the café later that afternoon at what she'd come to think of as his usual time.

He gave Elizabeth a warm smile and yawned. Almost immediately she yawned back and delivered a cup of coffee to his table.

"How do you feel?" he asked, his hand deliberately brushing hers.

"Tired. How about you?"

"Exhausted. I'm not used to these late nights and early mornings." He continued to hold her hand, his thumb stroking the inside of her wrist.

"And you think *I* am?" she teased.

His eyes widened for an instant. "Can I see you tonight?"

The idea of refusing never even occured to her. "Depends." No need to let him feel overconfident. "What do you have in mind?" She batted her eyelashes at him wickedly.

"Collecting on what's due me. Eight, I believe, is the correct number."

Four

The moon silently smiled down from the starlit heavens, casting its glow over the sandy beach. Breed and Peter had gathered driftwood, and blue tongues of fire flickered out from between the small, dry logs.

Elizabeth sat in the sand beside the fire and leaned against Breed, reveling in his quiet strength. His arms were wrapped around her from behind, enclosing her in his embrace. His breathing was even and undisturbed in the peace of the night. Communicating with words wasn't necessary. They'd been talking all week, often into the early hours of the morning. Now, words seemed unnecessary.

"I love this beach," she murmured, thinking how easy it would be to close her eyes and fall asleep in Breed's arms. "Ever since the first night you brought me here, I've come to think of this beach as ours."

His hold tightened measurably as he rubbed his jaw over the top of her head, mussing her wind-tossed hair all the more. Gently he lowered his head and kissed the side of her neck. "I'd say we're being generous sharing it with the world, wouldn't you?"

She snuggled deeper into his arms. "More than generous," she agreed.

The sound of Gilly's laughter came drifting down the beach. She and Peter had taken off running, playing some kind of teasing game. Elizabeth enjoyed it when the four of them did things together, but she was grateful for this time alone with Breed by the fire.

"Where do they get their energy?" she asked, having difficulty restraining a wide yawn. "I don't know about you, but I can't take another week like this."

"I always mean to get you home earlier," he murmured, his voice faintly tinged with guilt.

They'd gone out every night, and she hadn't once gotten home before midnight. Each time they promised one another they would make it an early night, but they hadn't met that goal once. The earliest she had crawled into bed had been twelve-thirty. Even then, she'd often lain awake and stared at the ceiling, thinking how dangerously close she was to falling in love with Breed.

"I wish I knew more about the constellations," she whispered, disliking the meandering trail of her thoughts. Love confused her. She had never been sure what elusive qualities distinguished love from infatuation. And if she did convince herself she was in love with Breed, would she ever be certain that it wasn't gratitude for the renewed lease on life he had so unwittingly given her? Tonight, in his arms, she could lie back and stare at the stars blazing in the black velvet sky. Only weeks ago she would have stumbled in the dark, unable to look toward the light. He had fixed that for her.

A hundred times she had flirted with the idea of telling him who she was. Each time, she realized that the knowledge would ruin their relationship. As it was, she would be faced with leaving him, Gilly and San Francisco soon enough.

She recognized that it was selfish to steal this brief happiness at the expense of others, but she couldn't help herself. It had been so long since she'd felt this good. Without even knowing it, Breed and Gilly had given her back the most precious gift of all: the ability to laugh and see beyond her grief. Being with them had lifted her from the mire of regret and self-pity. For that she would always be grateful.

"What's wrong?" Breed asked, tenderly brushing the hair from her temple.

His sensitivity to her moods astonished her. "What makes you ask?"

"You went tense on me for a moment."

She twisted so that she could lean back and study his ruggedly powerful face. His eyes were shadowed and unreadable, but she recognized the unrest in his look. Something was troubling him. She could sense it as strongly as she could feel the moisture of the ocean mist on her face. She'd recognized it in his eyes several times this past week. At first she'd thought it was her imagination. A yearning to understand him overcame her. "Things aren't always what they appear," she found herself saying. She hoped that he would trust her enough to tell her what was troubling him. But she wouldn't force his confidence.

Everything seemed to go still. Even the sound of the waves pounding against the beach faded. "What makes you say that?"

She resumed her former position, disappointed and a little hurt. Still, if Breed had secrets, so did she, and she certainly wasn't about to blurt out hers, so in all fairness, she shouldn't expect him to.

"Nothing." Her low voice was filled with resignation.

Slowly, tantalizingly, he ran his hands down her arms. "I have to go out of town next week."

"Oh." The word trembled on her lips with undisguised disappointment.

"I'll be flying out Monday, but I should be back sometime Tuesday," he explained.

"I'll miss you."

He drew her back against the unrestrained strength of his torso. "I wouldn't go if it wasn't necessary. You're right, you know." He spoke so low that she had to strain to hear him. "Things aren't always what they appear."

Later, when Breed had dropped her off at the apartment and she had settled in bed, his enigmatic words echoed in her mind. She couldn't imagine what was troubling him. But whatever it was, she sensed he was planning to settle it while he was out of town. He'd been quiet tonight. At first she had attributed his lack of conversation to how tired they both were. But it was more than that. She didn't know why she was so sure of it, but she was.

When she had first met Breed, she'd seen him only as muscular and handsome, two qualities she had attributed to shallow and self-centered men. But he had proved her wrong. This man was deep and intense. So intense that she often wondered what accounted for the powerful attraction that had brought them together.

A shadowy figure appeared in the doorway. "Are you asleep?" Gilly whispered.

Elizabeth sat up, bunching the pillows behind her back. "Not yet." She gestured toward the end of her bed, inviting her roommate to join her.

Gilly took a long swallow from a glass of milk and walked into the moonlit room, then sat on the edge of the bed. "I don't know what's wrong. I couldn't sleep, either."

"Did you have a good time tonight?" Elizabeth felt compelled to whisper, although there was no one there to disturb.

"I enjoy being with Peter," Gilly confessed with an exaggerated sigh, "but only as a friend."

"Is that a problem?"

Gilly's laugh was light and airy. "Not really, since I'm sure he feels the same way. It makes me wonder if I'll ever fall in love."

Elizabeth bit into her lip to keep from laughing out loud. "Do you realize how funny you sound? First you're happy because you and Peter are happy being just friends. Then you're disappointed because you aren't in love."

Gilly's smile was highlighted by the filtered light of the moon passing through the open window. "Yes, I suppose it does sound a little outrageous. I guess what I'd really like is to have the kind of relationship you and Breed share."

"He's a special man." Elizabeth spoke wistfully. Breed had taught her valuable lessons this past week. Without her long walk in the valley she might not have recognized the thrill of the mountaintop. Breed and Gilly had taught her to laugh and love life again. Life was beautiful in San Francisco. No wonder her mother had loved this city.

"I've seen the way he looks at you," Gilly continued, "and my heart melts. I want a man to feel that way about me."

"But not Peter."

"At this point I'm not choosy. I want to know what it's like to be in love. Really in love, like you and Breed."

"In love? Me and Breed?" Elizabeth tossed back the words in astonished disbelief.

"Yes, you and Breed," Gilly returned indignantly.

"You've got it all wrong." Elizabeth's thoughts were waging a fierce battle with one another. Gilly had to be mistaken. Breed couldn't be in love with her. She could only end up hurting him. The minute he learned about her wealth and position, he would feel betrayed and angry. She couldn't allow that to happen.

"We're attracted, but we're not in love," she returned adamantly, nodding once for emphasis.

The sound of Gilly's bemused laugh filled the room. "Honestly, how can anyone be so blind?"

"But Breed and I hardly know one another," Elizabeth argued. "What we feel at this point is infatuation, maybe, but no one falls in love in two weeks."

"Haven't you read *Romeo and Juliet?*" Gilly asked her accusingly. "People don't need a long courtship to know they're in love."

"Breed's a wonderful man, and I'd consider myself fortunate if he loved me." A thickening lump tightened her throat, making it impossible to talk for a moment. "But it's too soon for either of us to know what we really feel. Much too soon," Elizabeth reiterated.

Gilly was uncharacteristically quiet for a long moment. "Maybe I'm way off," she murmured thoughtfully. "But I don't think so. I have the feeling that once you admit what's going on inside your heart and your head, you won't be able to deny it."

"Perhaps not," Elizabeth murmured, troubled by Gilly's words.

"Are you seeing him tomorrow?"

"Not until the afternoon. He decided that after all the sleep I lost this week, I should sleep late tomorrow."

"But you're awake because you're lying here thinking about him. Right?" Gilly asked softly.

"No." Elizabeth yawned loudly, raising her arms high above her head. She hoped her friend would take the not-so-subtle message.

"And not being able to sleep doesn't tell you anything?" Gilly pressed.

"It tells me that I'd have a much easier time if a certain know-it-all wasn't sitting on the end of my bed, bugging the heck out of me." As much as she wanted to deny her friend's assessment, Elizabeth had been impressed more than once with Gilly's insight into people and situations. At twenty, she was wise beyond her years.

"I can take a hint, unlike certain people I know," Gilly said, bounding to her feet. "You wait, Elizabeth Wainwright. When you realize you're in love with Breed, your head's going to spin for a week."

Turning onto her side, Elizabeth scooted down and pulled the covers up to her chin. "Don't count on it," she mumbled into the pillow, forcing her eyes closed.

Standing beside the foot of the bed, Gilly finished the rest of her milk. "I'll see you in the morning," she said as she headed toward the door.

"Gilly." Elizabeth stopped her. "Breed's not really in love with me, is he?"

Staring pointedly at the ceiling, Gilly slowly shook her head in undisguised disgust. "I swear the girl's blind," she said to the light fixture, then turned back to Elizabeth. "Yes, Breed's head over heels in love with you. Only a fool wouldn't have guessed. Good night, fool."

"Good night," Elizabeth murmured with a sinking feeling. She'd been naive to believe that she could nurture this relationship and not pay an emotional price. She had to do something soon, before it was too late. If it wasn't already.

"All right," Breed said, breathing heavily. He tightened his grip on Hilda's steering wheel. "Out with it."

Elizabeth's face paled as she glanced out the side of the Jeep. The afternoon had been a disaster from the start, and all because of her and her ridiculous mood. She had hoped to speak honestly with Breed. She wanted to tell him that she was frightened by what was happening between them. At first she'd thought to suggest that he start seeing someone else, but the thought of him holding another woman had made her stomach tighten painfully. The crazy part was that she'd never thought of herself as the jealous type.

"Are you pouting because I'm going away? Is that the reason for the silent treatment?"

"No," she denied in a choked whisper. "That's not it." She kept her face averted, letting the wind whip her honey curls in every direction. She was so close to tears it was ludicrous.

When he pulled over to the curb and parked so he could face her, her heart sank to her knees. His gentle hand on her shoulder was nearly her undoing. She didn't want him to be gentle and concerned. If he were angry, it would be so much easier to explain her confused thoughts.

"Beth, what is it?"

Like Gilly, Breed had started calling her Beth. But it wasn't what he called her, it was the way he said it, the tender, almost loving way he let it roll from his lips. No name had ever sounded so beautiful.

Miserable, she placed her hand over his and turned around so that she could see his face. Of their own volition, her fingers rose to trace the angular lines of his proud jaw.

He emitted a low groan and took hold of her shoulders, putting some distance between them. "I have enough trouble keeping my hands off you without you doing that."

She dropped her hands, color rushing to her cheeks. "That's what's wrong," she said in a low voice she hardly recognized as her own. "I'm frightened, Breed."

"Of what?"

She swallowed back the uneasiness that filled her. "I'm worried that we're becoming too intense."

He dropped his hands and turned so that he was staring straight ahead. As if he needed something to do with his fingers, he gripped the steering wheel. She could tell that he was angry by the way his knuckles whitened. His look proved he didn't understand what she was saying.

"Things are getting too hot and heavy for you. Is that it?"

It wasn't, but she didn't know how else to explain her feelings. "Yes…yes they are."

"Then what you're saying is that you'd prefer it if we didn't see each other anymore?"

"No!" That thought was intolerable.

"The trouble with you is that you don't know what you want." The icy edge to his tone wrapped its way around her throat, choking off a reply.

He didn't appear to need one. Without hesitating, he turned the ignition key, and Hilda's engine roared to life. Jerking the gearshift, he pulled back onto the street.

"I feel we both need time to think." She practically had to shout to be heard above the noise of the traffic. Breed didn't answer. Before she could think of another way to explain herself, he had pulled up in front of her brick apartment building. He left the engine running.

"I agree," he said, his voice emotionless. "We've been seeing too much of one another."

"You've misunderstood everything I've said," she murmured miserably, wishing she had explained herself better.

"I don't think so," he replied, his jaw tightening. "I'll call you Tuesday, after I get back to town. That is, if you want to hear from me again."

"Of course I do." Frustration rocked her. "I'm sorry I said anything. I don't want you to go away angry."

He hesitated, and although he didn't say anything for several moments, she could feel the resentment fade. The air between them became less oppressive, lighter. "The thing is, you're right," he admitted tightly. "Both of us needed to be reminded of that. Take care of yourself while I'm away."

"I will," she whispered.

"I'll phone you Tuesday."

"Tuesday," she agreed, climbing out of the car. She stood on the sidewalk as he pulled away and merged with the flowing traffic.

A flick of her wrist turned the key that allowed her into the apartment. Gilly was sitting on the sofa, reading a romance novel and munching on a carrot. "How did everything go?" she asked.

"Fine," Elizabeth responded noncommittally. But she felt miserable. Her talk with Breed hadn't settled anything. Instead of clearing the air, it had only raised more questions. Now she was left with three days to sort through her thoughts and decide how she could continue to see him and not complicate their relationship by falling in love.

"If everything's so wonderful, why do you look like you're going to burst into tears?"

Elizabeth tried to smile, but the effort failed miserably. "Because I am."

"I take it you don't want to talk."

It was all Elizabeth could manage to shake her head.

Later that evening, as the sun was sinking low into a lavender sky, Gilly dressed for an evening out. Her cousin was getting married, and her parents expected her to attend the wedding although she never had cared for this particular cousin.

"Are you sure you won't come?" Gilly asked Elizabeth for the sixth time.

"I'm sure," Elizabeth responded from the kitchen table, making an exaggerated stroke along the side of her nail with a file. Fiddling with her fingernails had given the appearance she was busy and untroubled. But she doubted that her smoke screen had fooled Gilly. "I thought you'd conned Peter into going with you?"

"I regret that," Gilly said with frank honesty.

"Why?" Elizabeth glanced down at her collection of nail polish.

"Knowing my dad, he's probably going to make a big deal about my bringing Peter. This whole thing's going to end up embarrassing us both. I hate being forced to attend something just because it's family."

Elizabeth cast her a sympathetic look. She'd suffered through enough family obligations to empathize with her friend's feelings.

Gilly and Peter left soon afterward, and she finished her nails, wondering if Breed would notice when she saw him next. She watched television for a while, keeping her mind off him. But not for long.

She picked up the paperback Gilly had been reading, and quickly read the first couple of chapters, surprised at how much she was enjoying the book. The next thing she knew, Gilly was shaking her awake and telling her to climb into bed or she would get a crick in her neck.

It was the middle of the morning when she woke again. Feeling out of sorts and cranky, she read the morning paper and did the weekly grocery shopping. When Gilly suggested a drive, she declined. Not until later did she realize that she'd been waiting for Breed to phone, even though he'd said he wouldn't, and was keenly disappointed when he didn't.

Monday evening, when her cell did ring she all but flew across the room in her eagerness to grab it from her purse. She desperately wanted it to be Breed. But it wasn't. Instead, she found herself talking to her disgruntled father.

"I haven't heard from you in a while. Are you okay?"

"Of course I am." Although disappointment coated her voice, she had to admit she was pleased to hear from her father. She was even more grateful that Gilly was taking a shower and wasn't likely to overhear the conversation. "I'm happy, Dad, for the first time since Mom died."

"I was thinking about this job of yours. Are you still working as a…waitress?" He said the word as though he found it distasteful.

"Yes, and I'm enjoying it."

"I've been talking to some friends of mine," he said in a tone that told her he was anxious about her. "If you feel you need to work, then we could get you on at the embassy. Your French is excellent."

"Dad," she interrupted, "I like it at the Patisserie. Don't worry about me."

"But as a common waitress?" The contemptuous disbelief was back in his voice again. "I want so much more for you, Princess." Her father hadn't called her that since she was thirteen. "When are you coming home? I think it might be a good idea if you were here."

"Dad," she said impatiently, "for the first time in months I'm sleeping every night. I'm eager for each new morning. I'm happy, really happy. Don't ruin that."

She could hear her father's uncertainty, feel his indecision. "Have you met someone special?" he said.

The question was a loaded one, and she wasn't sure how to respond, especially in light of her discussion with Breed. "Yes and no."

"Meaning…?" he pressed.

"I've made some friends. Good friends. What makes you ask?"

"No reason. I just don't want you to do something you'll regret later."

"Like what?" Indignation caused her voice to rise perceptibly.

"I don't know." He paused and exhaled forcefully. "Siggy's phoned for you several times."

Elizabeth released an inward groan. Siegfried Winston Chamberlain III was the most boring stuffed shirt she'd ever known. More than that, she had openly disliked him from the day a small, helpless bird had flown into a freshly washed window and broken its neck. The look in Siggy's eyes revealed that he'd enjoyed witnessing its death. From that time on she'd avoided him. But he had pursued her relentlessly from their teenage years, though she was certain he wasn't in love with her. She wasn't even sure he liked her. What she did recognize was the fact that a union between their two families would be financially expedient to the Chamberlains.

"Tell Siggy the same thing you told him when I was in Paris."

"Siggy loves you."

"Dad…" Elizabeth didn't want to lose her temper, not on the phone, when it would be difficult to settle their differences. "I honestly don't think Siggy knows what love is. I've got to go. I'll phone you next week. Now, don't worry about me. Promise?"

"You'll phone next week? Promise?"

She successfully repressed a sharp reply. Her father had never shown such concern for her welfare. He was acting as though she was working undercover for the CIA.

Honestly, she mused irritably. Would she ever understand her father?

"You miss him, don't you?" Gilly asked her later that evening.

Elizabeth didn't even try to pretend. She knew Gilly was referring to Breed. She had confided in her friend, and was again grateful for Gilly's insight and understanding. He had been on her mind all weekend. Monday had dragged, and she was counting the hours until she heard from him again. "I do," she admitted readily. "I wish I'd never said anything."

Gilly nodded sympathetically.

But it was more than missing Breed, Elizabeth thought to herself. Much more. For three days it had been as though a vital part of her was missing. The realization frightened her. He had come to mean more to her in a few weeks than anyone she'd known. Gilly, too. As she'd explained to her father, she was making friends. Maybe the first real friends of her life. But Breed was more than a friend, and it had taken this separation to prove it.

Tuesday Elizabeth kept taking out her cell to see if she had missed his call.

"From the look of you, someone might think you're waiting to hear from someone," Gilly teased.

"Am I that obvious?"

"Is the sun bright? Do bees buzz?" Gilly sat on the chair opposite Elizabeth. "Why not call him? Women do that these days, you know."

Elizabeth hesitated long enough to consider the idea. "I don't know."

"Well, it isn't going to hurt anything. His pride's been bruised. Besides, anything's better than having you mope around the apartment another night."

"I do not mope."

Gilly tried unsuccessfully to disguise a smile. "If you say so."

Elizabeth waited until nine for Breed to phone. She could call him, but seeing him in person would be so much better. Maybe Gilly was right and, despite what he'd said about calling her, he was waiting for her to contact him. She wouldn't sleep tonight unless she made the effort to see him. It wouldn't do any good to try to fool herself otherwise.

"I think I'll go for a walk," she announced brightly, knowing she wasn't fooling her friend.

"Tonight's perfect for a stroll," Gilly murmured, not taking her attention from the television, but Elizabeth noticed the way the corners of her eyes crinkled as she struggled not to reveal her amusement. "I don't suppose you want me to wait up for you."

With a bemused smile, Elizabeth closed the door, not bothering to answer.

There were plenty of reasons that could explain why Breed hadn't called. Maybe his trip had been extended. He might not even be home. But as Gilly had pointedly stated, the evening *was* perfect for a stroll. The sun had set below a cloudless horizon and darkness had blanketed the city. The streets were alive with a variety of people. Elizabeth didn't notice much of what was going on around her. Her quick, purpose-filled strides took her the three blocks to Breed's apartment in a matter of a few short minutes. She had never been there, yet the address was burned into her memory.

For all her resolve, when she saw the light under his door, her heart sank. Breed was home and hadn't contacted her.

Her first light knock went unnoticed, so she pressed the buzzer long and hard.

"Beth!" Breed sounded shocked when he opened the door.

"So you made it back safely after all," she said, aware of the faintly accusatory note in her voice. He must have realized that she would be waiting for his call. "What time did you get back?" The minute the question slipped from her lips, she regretted having asked. Her coming was obvious enough.

"About six." He stepped back, silently and grudgingly issuing the invitation for her to come inside.

She was surprised at how bare the apartment looked. The living area displayed nothing that stamped the apartment with his personality. There were no pictures on the walls, or books and magazines lying around. The place seemed sterile, it was so clean. It looked as if he'd just moved in.

"I thought you said you would phone."

"I wasn't sure you wanted to hear from me."

Without waiting for an invitation, she sat on the sofa and crossed her long legs, hoping to give a casual impression.

He took a chair on the other side of the room and leaned forward, his elbows resting on his knees. There was a coiled alertness about him that he was attempting to disguise. But Elizabeth knew him too well. In the same way that he was sensitive to her, she was aware of him. He seemed to be waiting for her to speak.

"I missed you," she said softly, hoping her words would release the tension in the room. "More than I ever thought I would."

He straightened and looked uncomfortable. "Yes. Well, that's only natural. We've been seeing a lot of each other the last couple of weeks."

Her fingers were laced together so tightly that they began to ache. She unwound them and flexed her hands before standing and moving to the window on the far side of the room. "It's more than that," she announced with her back to him. Deliberately she turned, then leaned back with her hands resting on the windowsill. "Nothing seemed right without you...."

Breed vaulted to his feet. "Beth, listen to me. We're tired. It's been a long day. I think we should both sleep on this." His look was an odd mixture of tenderness and impatience. "Come on, I'll drive you home."

"No." She knew a brush-off when she heard one. He didn't want her here; that much was obvious. He hadn't been himself from the moment she set foot in the door. "I walked here, I'll walk back."

"All right, I'll come with you." The tone of his voice told her he would brook no argument.

She lifted one shoulder in a half-shrug. "It's a free country."

He relaxed the minute he locked the door. There was something inside the apartment he hadn't wanted her to see, she realized. Not a woman hiding in his bedroom; she was sure of that. Amusement drifted across her face and awoke a slow smile.

"What's so funny?" he wanted to know.

"Nothing."

His hand gripped hers. "Come on, and I'll introduce you to BART."

She paused midstride, making him falter slightly. With her hands positioned challengingly on her hips, she glared defiantly at him. "Oh, no, you don't, Andrew Breed. If you don't want to see me again, then fine. But I won't have you introducing me to other men. I can find my own dates, thank you."

A crooked smile slashed his face as he turned toward her, his eyes hooded.

"Bay Area Rapid Transit. BART is the subway."

"Oh." She felt ridiculous. The natural color of her cheeks was heightened with embarrassment.

"So you missed me," he said casually as they strolled along the busy sidewalk. "That's nice to know."

She greeted his words with silence. First he had shunned her, and now he was making fun of her. Other than a polite "good night" when they arrived at her building, she didn't have anything to say to him. The whole idea of going to him had been idiotic. Well, she'd learned her lesson.

"The thing is, I discovered I missed you, too."

Again she didn't respond.

"But missing someone is a strange thing," he continued. "There are varying degrees. Like after your mother died, I imagine…"

Elizabeth felt a chill rush over her skin that had nothing to do with the light breeze. "I never told you my mother was dead," she said stiffly.

Five

"You don't mind, do you?" Gilly asked contritely. "I wouldn't have mentioned your mother to Breed if I'd known you objected."

"No, don't worry about it," Elizabeth said gently, shaking her head.

"Even though Breed and I went out several times before you started dating him, I knew from the beginning that he was really only interested in you. From the first date you were all he talked about."

Breed had explained to Elizabeth yesterday that Gilly had told him about her mother. Yet she'd doubted him. Everything about last night remained clouded in her mind. From the moment she'd entered his apartment, she had felt like an unwelcome intruder. None of his actions made sense, and her suspicions had begun to cross the line into outright paranoia.

"Peter and I are going to dinner and a movie," Gilly said, changing the subject.

"I have some shopping I want to do," Elizabeth returned absently.

Not until later that evening, when she was facing the store detective, did she remember that she couldn't phone Gilly, whose cell would be off in the theater, and have her come. A heaviness pressed against her heart, and she struggled to maintain her composure as the balding man led her toward the department store office.

She walked past the small crowd that had gathered near her and saw a tall, familiar figure on the far side of the floor in the men's department.

"Breed!" she called, thanking heaven that he had chosen this day to shop.

He turned at the sound of her voice, his brows lowering. "Beth, what is it?"

She bit into her bottom lip, more embarrassed than she could ever remember being. "Someone stole my purse. I haven't got any way to get home or a key to the apartment."

Elizabeth's face was buried in her hands when Breed delivered a steaming cup of coffee to the kitchen table where she sat. The manager had let her into the apartment, but she still had so much to deal with to straighten everything out that the feeling was overwhelming.

"Tell me again what happened," Breed said as he straddled a chair beside her.

She shook her head. Everything important was inside her purse. Her money, credit cards, cell phone, identification. Everything. Gone in a matter of seconds. As crazy as it sounded, she felt as if she had been personally violated. She was both stunned and angry.

"I don't want to talk about it," she replied stiffly. What she wanted was for Breed to leave so she could be alone.

"Beth." He said her name so gently that she closed her eyes to the emotion he aroused in her. "Honey, I can't help unless I know what happened."

One tear broke past the thick dam of her lashes and flowed unrestrained down her pale face. Resolutely, she wiped it aside.

"I decided to do a little shopping after work. Peter had picked up Gilly, and they were going out, and I didn't want to go home to an empty house." Breed hadn't mentioned anything last night about getting together, and she didn't want to sit around in an empty apartment missing him.

"Go on," he encouraged. He continued to hold her hand, his thumb stroking the inside of her wrist in a soothing action that at any other time would have been sensuous and provocative.

"I'd only bought a couple of things and decided to stop in the rest room before taking BART home. I set my purse and the packages on the counter while I washed. I turned to dry my hands. When I turned back, my purse, the packages… everything was gone. I was so stunned, I didn't know what to do."

"You must have seen something."

"That's what Detective Beaman thought. But I didn't. I didn't even hear anything." She paused, reliving the short seconds. She could tell them nothing.

Even now, an hour later, sitting in her kitchen, a feeling of disbelief filled her.

This couldn't really be happening. This was a bad dream, and when she woke, everything would be fine again. At least that was what she desperately wanted to believe.

"What did they take?"

"Breed, don't. Please. I can't talk about it anymore. I just want to take a bath and pretend this never happened." Later she would have to contact her father. It didn't take much of an imagination to know what his response was going to be. He would insist she leave San Francisco, and then they would argue. She let the unpleasant thoughts fade. She didn't want to think about it.

Breed released her wrist and stood. His hands were positioned on his lean hips, his expression grim and unyielding. "Beth," he insisted in a low, coaxing tone. "Think. There's something you're not remembering. Something small.

Close your eyes and go over every minute of the time you were shopping."

She clenched her teeth to keep from yelling. "Don't you think I haven't already?" she said with marked impatience. "Every detail of every minute has been playing back repeatedly in my mind."

He exhaled sharply, letting her know his patience was as limited as her own.

She stared pointedly at the bare surface of the table, which blurred as the welling tears collected in her eyes. She managed to restrain their fall, but she couldn't keep her chin from trembling. Tears were a sign of weakness, and the Wainwrights frowned on signs of weakness.

Breed sighed as he eliminated the distance between them and stood behind her. Gently he comforted her by massaging her shoulders and neck. The demanding pressure of his fingers half lifted her from the chair, forcing her to stand.

She held herself stiffly, angry. "This is your fault," she whispered in a faintly hysterical tone.

"Mine?" He turned her around. His amber eyes narrowed into thin slits.

She didn't need him to tell her how unreasonable she was being, but she couldn't help herself. Her tears blurred his expression as she lashed out at him bitterly. "Why were you so unwelcoming last night? Why didn't you want me at your apartment? Not to mention that you said you'd call and then you didn't." She inhaled shakily. "Don't bother to deny it. I'm not stupid. I know when I'm not wanted. And why...why didn't you come into the café today?" Her accusations were fired as quick as machine gun bullets.

He groaned as his hands cupped her face. Anger flashed across his features, then vanished. "There wasn't a single

minute that you weren't on my mind."
Self-derisive anger darkened his eyes.

"Then why…?" Her heart fluttered uncertainly, excited and yet afraid.

Motionless, he held her, revealing none of his thoughts. "Because," he admitted as the smoldering light of desire burned in his eyes. His hand slid slowly along the back of her waist, bringing her infinitesimally closer.

When he fitted his mouth to hers, a small, happy sound escaped from her throat. His thick arms around her waist lifted her from the kitchen floor. Her softness was molded to his male length as he kissed her until her lips were swollen and trembling.

"I missed you so much," she admitted, wrapping her arms around his neck. "I was so afraid you didn't want to see me again."

"Not want to see you?" he repeated. His husky tone betrayed his frustration.

"You confuse me. I don't know what kind of game you're playing."

Anxiously, she brushed the hair from his face and kissed him, her lips exploring the planes and contours of his angular features with short, teasing kisses. "I'm not playing any game," she whispered.

He loosened his grip so that her feet touched the floor once again. "No games?" Amusement was carved in the lines of his face. "I don't believe that."

Deliberately she directed his mouth to hers and kissed him long and slow, her lips moving sensuously over his.

He broke the contact and held her at arm's length as he took several deep breaths.

"What's wrong?" she whispered. She didn't want him to pull away from her. A chill seeped through her bloodstream as she tried to decipher his attitude. The messages he sent her were confused. He wanted to be with her, but he didn't. He liked coming to her apartment but didn't want her at his. His kisses affected her as much as they affected him, yet he pulled away whenever things became too intense.

The phone rang, and he dropped his hands and stared at it as if it were an intruder. "Do you want me to answer it?" he questioned.

She shook her head and answered it herself. "Hello." She couldn't disguise the soft tremble in her voice. "Yes, yes, this is Elizabeth Wainwright."

Breed brushed his fingers through his hair as he paced the room.

"Yes, yes," she repeated breathlessly. "I did lose my purse." Not until the conversation was half over did the words sink into her consciousness.

"Breed!" she cried excitedly as she replaced the receiver. "They've found my purse!"

"Who did?" He turned her in his arms, his tense features relaxing.

"The store. That was them on the phone. Apparently whoever took it was only after the cash. Someone turned it in to the office only a few minutes ago after finding it in the stairway."

"Your credit cards and identification?"

"There. All they took was the cash."

He hauled her into his arms and released a heavy sigh that revealed his relief. Her own happy sigh joined his. "They said I should come and pick it up. Let's go right away," she said, laughing. "I feel naked without my purse." Giddy with relief, she waltzed around the room until he captured her and swung her in the air as if she weighed no more than a doll.

"Feel better?"

"Oh, yes!" she exclaimed, kissing him lightly. "Can we go now?"

"I think we should." He laced his fingers through hers, then lifted their joined hands to his lips and kissed the back of her hand.

He locked the apartment with the spare key the manager had given her and tucked it into his pocket. Hand in hand, they walked outside.

She patted Hilda's seat cushion as she got in. "You know what I thought last night?" she asked as Breed revved the engine.

He turned and smiled warmly at her. "I can't imagine." His finger lingered longer than necessary as it removed a long strand of silken hair that the wind had blown across her happy face.

"For one fleeting instant I was convinced you were hiding a woman in your bedroom." At the shocked look he gave her, she broke into delighted giggles.

"Beth." Thick lines marred his smooth brow. "Whatever made you suspect something like that?"

Pressing her head against his shoulder, she released a contented sigh. "I don't know." She *did* know, but she wanted to relish this moment. Yesterday's ghosts were buried. Today's happiness shone brightly before her. Her joy was complete. "Forward, Hilda. Take me to my purse."

Breed merged with the heavy flow of traffic. "I suppose you're going to insist on celebrating."

"Absolutely."

"Dinner?"

She sat up and placed her hand on his where it rested on the gearshift. She had to keep touching him to believe that all this was real. "Yes, I'm starved. I don't think I've eaten all day."

"Why not?" He gave her a questioning glance.

She poked his stomach. "You know why."

He reclaimed her hand, and again he

kissed her fingers. She had the sensation he felt exactly as she did and couldn't keep his hands off her.

"What did Beaman say?"

"It wasn't Beaman. He said his name, but I can't remember it now."

"What did he say?" Breed glanced briefly in her direction.

"Just that I should come right away."

"That you should come right away." He drawled the words slowly. Then he dropped her hand and tightened his hold on the steering wheel as he glanced in the rearview mirror. The tires screeched as he made a U-turn in the middle of the street. The unexpected action caused Hilda to teeter for an instant.

"Breed!" Elizabeth screamed, holding on to the padded bar on the dash. "What is it? What's wrong?"

He didn't answer her as he weaved in and out of the traffic, blaring his horn impatiently. When they pulled up in front of her apartment again, he looked around and tensed.

She had no idea what had gotten into him. "Breed?" She tried a second time to talk to him. He sat alert and stiff. The look in his eyes was frightening. She had never seen anything more menacing.

"Call the police," he told her as he jumped from the Jeep.

"But, Breed—"

"Now. Hurry."

Confused, she jumped out, too. "What am I supposed to tell them?" she asked as she followed him onto the sidewalk and reached for his hand.

He pushed her arm away. "That wasn't the store that called," he explained impatiently. "It was whoever took your purse, and they're about to rob you blind."

"How do you know?" Nothing made sense anymore. Breed was like a dangerous stranger. Rage contorted his features until she hardly recognized him.

He grabbed her shoulders, his fingers biting mercilessly into her flesh. "Look." He jerked his head toward a moving van parked in front of the building. "Do as I say and call 9-1-1," he ordered in a threatening voice. "And don't come into the apartment until after the police arrive. Now go."

"Breed..." Panic filled her as he walked toward the door. "Don't go in there!" she shouted frantically, running after him. He was so intent that he didn't hear her. His glance of surprise when she grabbed his arm was quickly replaced with an angry scowl. "Get out of here."

With fear dictating her actions, she ran across the street to the safety of a beauty salon. She was sure the women thought she was crazy when she pulled out her cell, dialed the emergency police number, and reported a robbery in progress, all the while staring out through the large front window.

Like a caged animal, she paced the sidewalk outside her apartment, waiting for the patrol car. She held both hands over her mouth as she looked up and down the street. Everything was taking so long. Each second was an hour, every minute a lifetime. Not until the first police vehicle pulled up did she realize how badly she was trembling.

"In there," she said, and gave them her apartment number. "My boyfriend went up to stop them."

Another police car arrived, and while one officer went into the building on the heels of the first two, the other stayed outside and questioned her. At first she stared at him blankly, her mind refusing to concentrate on her own responses. Her answers were clipped, one-word replies.

Fifteen minutes later, two men and a woman were led out of the building by the police. Breed followed, talking to an officer. He paused long enough to search out Elizabeth in the growing crowd and smile reassuringly.

Her answering smile was shaky, but she felt her heart regain its normal rhythm. Her eyes followed him as he spoke to one officer and then another. When he joined her a few minutes later, he slipped an arm around her waist with familiar ease. Her fears evaporated at his touch.

"Do you recognize any of them?" he asked her.

Lamely, she nodded. "The woman was in the elevator with me, but she didn't go into the rest room."

"But she got off on the same floor?"

She wasn't sure. "I don't remember, but she must have."

"It doesn't matter if you remember or not. There's enough evidence here to lock them up." His arm remained on her waist as he directed her inside.

"How'd you know?" Dazed and almost

tongue-tied, she stared up at him. "What clued you in to what was going on?"

"To be honest, I don't know," he admitted. "Something didn't ring true. First, it wasn't Beaman who phoned, and then there was something about the way you were instructed to come right away. They were probably waiting within sight of the building and watched us leave."

"But how'd they know my address and phone number?" All her identification listed her Boson address. Even her driver's license was from Massachusetts. There hadn't been any reason to obtain a California license, since she didn't have a car and was only planning on staying for the summer.

"Your name, address, and telephone number are printed on your checks."

She groaned. "Of course."

"We need to go to the police station and fill out a few forms. Are you up to that?"

"I'm fine. But I want to know about you. What happened in there?"

"Nothing much." It didn't sound like he wanted to talk about it. "I counted on the element of surprise."

"Yes, but there were three of them." She wasn't about to let the subject drop. "How did you defend yourself?"

His wide shoulders tensed as he hesitated before answering. "I've studied the martial arts."

"Breed!" she exclaimed. "Really? You should have said something." The longer she was with him, the more she realized how little she actually knew about him. She had actually avoided asking too many questions, afraid of revealing too much about herself. But she wouldn't shy away from them anymore.

Gilly and Peter returned to the apartment chatting happily.

Elizabeth glanced up and sighed.

"Where were you when I needed you?" she teased her roommate.

"When did you need me?"

"Today. Someone took my purse."

"They did more than that," Breed repeated with a trace of anger.

"What happened?" Peter looked incredulous. "I think you better start at the beginning."

Slowly, shaking her head, Elizabeth sighed. "Let me explain."

An hour later Breed glanced pointedly at his wristwatch and held out his hand to Elizabeth. "Walk me to the door." The quiet firmness of his request and the tender look in his eyes sent her pulse racing.

"Sure," she said, eagerly moving around the sofa to his side.

He waited until they reached the entryway to turn her into his arms. Her back was supported by the panels of the door. His hands were on each side of her head as his gaze roamed slowly over her upturned face. For one heart-stopping second his eyes rested on her parted lips; his look was as potent as a physical touch.

"I want to see you tomorrow."

She released a heavy sigh. "Oh, thank goodness," she said, offering him a brilliant smile. "I was afraid I was going to be forced to ask *you* out."

His look grew dark and serious. "You'd do that?"

"Yes." She didn't trust herself to add an explanation.

He pulled his gaze from hers. "Would you like to go fishing?"

"You mean with poles and hooks and worms?"

"I've got a sailboat. We could leave tomorrow afternoon, once you're off work."

"Can I bring anything?"

"The worms," Breed teased.

"Try again, buddy. How about some sandwiches?" She could have Evelyn make some up for her before she left the Patisserie tomorrow.

"Fine."

Breed's kiss was disappointingly short but immeasurably sweet. Long after he left, she felt his presence linger. Twice she turned and started to say something to him before realizing he'd left for the evening.

Elizabeth felt Gilly's curious stare as she came out of the bedroom the following afternoon.

"Where's Breed taking you, for heaven's sake? You look like you just finished plowing the back forty."

Self-consciously, Elizabeth looked down at her tennis shoes and the faded jeans that were rolled midway up her calf. The shirttails of her red-checkered blouse were tied loosely at her midriff.

"Fishing. I'm not overdressed, am I? I have my swimsuit on underneath."

"You look…" One side of Gilly's mouth quirked upward as she paused, her face furrowed in concentration. "Different," she concluded.

"I'll admit I don't usually dress like this, but—"

"It's not the clothes," Gilly interrupted. "There's a certain aura about you. A look in your eye."

Turning, Elizabeth found a mirror and examined herself closely. "You're crazy. I'm no different than I was last week—or last night, for that matter."

Gilly ignored her and paid excessive attention to the crossword puzzle she was doing.

"No quick reply?" Elizabeth asked teasingly. She was used to doing verbal battle with her roommate.

Gilly bit into the eraser at the end of the pencil. "Not me. I learned a long time ago that it's better not to argue with you."

But she rolled her eyes when she thought Elizabeth wasn't looking.

Breed arrived just then, and Elizabeth didn't have the opportunity to banter further with Gilly. If there was something different about her, as her friend believed, then it was because she was happier, more complete.

Outside the building, Elizabeth scanned the curb for Hilda, but the Jeep wasn't parked within sight.

"Here." Breed held open the door to a silver sedan, the same car he'd driven before introducing her to Hilda.

"Where's Hilda?"

"Home." Breed's reply was abrupt.

"Good grief, how many cars have you got?"

The smile that lifted the corners of his mouth looked forced. "One too many," he answered cryptically.

She wanted to question him further, but he closed her door and walked around to the driver's side. He paused and glanced warily at the street before climbing inside the car.

"Are you planning on kidnapping me?" she teased.

For an instant his sword-sharp gaze pinned her against the seat. "What makes you ask something as crazy as that?" Impatience sounded in his crisp voice.

She had meant it as a joke, so she was surprised that he had taken her seriously. She arched one delicately shaped brow at his defensive tone and cocked her head. "What's gotten into you?"

"Nothing."

Releasing her breath slowly, she gazed out the side window, watching as the scenery whipped past. From the minute he had asked her on this outing, she had been looking forward to their time together. She didn't want anything to ruin it.

At the marina, his heavy steps sounded

ominously as he led her along the long wooden dock toward his sailboat. But his mood altered once they were slicing through the water, the multicolored spinnaker bloated with wind. Content, she dragged her fingers in the darkish green waters of San Francisco Bay, delighting in the cool feel against her hand, while Breed sat behind her at the tiller.

"This is wonderful!" she shouted. But he couldn't hear her, because a gust of wind carried her voice forward. Laughing, she scooted closer, rose to her knees and spoke directly into his ear, smiling.

His returning smile revealed his own enjoyment. He relaxed against the gunnel, his long legs stretched out and crossed at the ankles. With one hand he managed the tiller as he motioned with the other for Elizabeth to sit at his side.

She did so willingly.

When he reached a spot that apparently met his specifications, he lowered the sails and dropped anchor.

Giving her nothing more than the basic instructions, he baited her hook and handed her a fishing pole.

"Now what?" She sat straight-backed and unsure as he readied his own pole and lowered the line into the deep waters on the opposite side of the boat.

"We wait for a hungry fish to come along and take a nibble."

"What if they're not hungry?"

"Are you always this much trouble?" he asked her, chuckling at her indignant look. "Your freckles are flashing at me again."

Involuntarily she brushed at her nose, as though her fingers could rub the tan flecks away. She was about to make a feisty retort when she felt a slight tug on her line.

"Breed," she whispered frantically. "I...I think I've got one." The pole dipped dramatically, nearly catching her off guard. "What do I do?" she cried, looking back to him, her eyes unsure.

"Reel it in."

"I can't," she said, silently pleading with him to take the pole from her. She should have known better.

"Sure you can," he assured her calmly. To offer her moral support, he reeled in his own line and went over to her, encouraging her as she struggled to bring in the fish.

She couldn't believe how much of a battle one small fish could wage. "What have I caught?" she shouted in her excitement. "A whale?" Perspiration broke out across her forehead as she pulled back on the pole and reeled in the fish inch by inch.

When the line snapped and she staggered backward, Breed caught her at the shoulders. "You all right?"

"No, darn it, I wanted that fish. What happened?"

He looked unconcerned and shrugged. "Any number of things. Want to try again?"

"Of course," she replied indignantly. He seemed to think she was a quitter, and she would like nothing better than to prove him wrong.

With her line back in the bay, Elizabeth leaned against the side, lazily enjoying the sun and wind. "Have you ever stopped to think that after all the times we've gone out, we still hardly know anything about each other?" she asked.

Her statement was met with silence. "What's there to know?"

She was treading on dangerous ground, and she knew it. Her relationship with Breed had progressed to the point where she felt he had a right to know who she was. But fear and indecision prevented her from broaching the subject boldly. "There's lots I'd like to know about you."

"Like what?" There was the slightest pause before his mouth thinned. He didn't seem overly eager to reveal more of himself.

"Well, for one thing…your family." If she led into the subject, then maybe he would ask her about hers, and she could explain bits and pieces of her background until things added up in his mind, since telling him outright was bound to be fatal to their promising relationship.

"Not much to tell you there. I'm the oldest of four boys. My great-grandfather came to California from Germany in search of lumber. He died here and left the land to his son." He paused and glanced at her. "What about you?"

She pressed her lips tightly together. For all her desire for honesty and despite her earlier resolution, when it came time to reveal the truth about her family, she found she couldn't. The bright, healthy color the wind and the sun had given her cheeks was washed swiftly away, leaving her unnaturally pale.

"I've got one older brother, Charlie." She swallowed tightly. "I don't think you'd like him."

"Why not?"

She lifted one petite shoulder. "He's… well, he's something of a stuffed shirt."

"Lawyer type."

She nodded, wanting to change the subject. "How much longer before I lure another fish to my bait?"

"Patience," Breed said, his back to her.

Her eyes fluttered closed. Her heart was pounding so hard she was sure he would notice. Unwittingly, he had given good advice. She had to be patient. Someday soon, when the time was right, she would tell him everything.

Six

The stars were twinkling like diamond chips in an ebony sky. The water lapped lightly against the side of Breed's boat, which, sails lowered, rocked gently in the murky water of San Francisco Bay. Four pairs of eager eyes gazed into the night sky, anticipating the next rocket burst to explode into a thousand shooting stars and briefly light up the heavens.

"I love the Fourth of July," Elizabeth murmured. Breed sat beside her, his arm draped casually over her shoulder. Gilly and Peter sat on the other side of the boat, holding hands. They might not be in love, but as Gilly had explained, they were certainly good friends.

One burst after another brightened the sky. Breed had said something earlier that week about going to Candlestick Park to watch the fireworks, but once the four of them had piled into Breed's sedan, they discovered that the traffic heading for the park was horrendous. He'd suggested that they take his sailboat into the bay and observe the fireworks from there, instead, an idea that had been met with enthusiasm by the others.

For nearly a week Breed had taken Elizabeth out on his boat every night after work. Sometimes they fished, depending on how much time they had and what their plans were afterward. He had led her forward a couple of times to raise and lower the sails. She loved to sail as much as he did, and the time they shared on the water had become the high point of her day. They talked openly, argued over politics, discussed books. He challenged her ideas on conservation and pollution, forcing her to stop and think about things she had previously accepted because of what she'd been told by others. Gently, but firmly, he made her form her own opinions. And she loved him for it.

She hadn't told him that she loved him, of course. The emotion was new to her and frightened her a little. The love she'd experienced in the past for her family and friends had been a mixture of respect and admiration. The only person with whom she had ever shared such a close relationship had been her mother. Of course, she would have grieved if her father had been the one who had suffered the stroke and died. But her mother had been her soulmate.

The love she felt for Breed went beyond friendship. Her love was fiery and intense, and the physical desire was sometimes overwhelming. Yet the joy she felt in his arms exceeded desire. Yes, she wanted him. More than that, she wanted to give herself to him. He must have known that, but he never allowed their lovemaking to go beyond a certain point. She didn't know why he was holding himself back. Not that she minded; that aspect of their relationship was only a small part of her feelings. When they could speak openly and honestly about their feelings and their commitment to one another, then they could deal with the physical aspect of their relationship. Her love went so much deeper. In analyzing her feelings, she thought that they also met on a higher plane, a spiritual one. Perhaps because of that, he felt it was too soon to talk about certain things. In some ways, they didn't need to.

She often wanted to talk to Gilly about her feelings, but she wasn't sure her friend, who was so much younger, would understand. If her mother had been alive, Elizabeth could have spoken to her. But she wasn't, and Elizabeth was forced to keep the inexplicable intensity of this relationship buried deep within her heart.

The only thing that marred her happiness was the sensation that something was troubling Breed. She'd tried to question him once and run up against a granite wall. Lately he'd been brooding and thoughtful. Although he hadn't said anything, she was fairly certain he'd lost his job. His hours had been flexible in the past, but lately he'd been coming into the Patisserie at all hours. Some days he even came in the morning and then again in the afternoon. Another thing she'd noticed was that they rarely ate in restaurants anymore. All the things they did together were inexpensive. Every Sunday they returned to Sigmund Stern Grove for the free concert. They took long walks on the beach and sailed almost daily. His apparent financial problems created others, effectively killing her desire to tell him about her background. How could she talk about her family's money without sounding insensitive? She had no doubt that the information could ruin what they shared.

When she glanced up from her musings she noted that Peter's arm was around Gilly, who had her head pressed against his shoulder. The look in Gilly's eyes seemed troubled, although Elizabeth realized she could have misread it in the reflected moonlight.

"Gilly, are you feeling okay?" she felt obliged to ask.

Gilly straightened. "Of course. Why shouldn't I be?"

"You're so quiet."

"I think we should enjoy the novelty," Peter interjected. "Once ol' motor-mouth gets going, it's hard to shut her up."

"Motor-mouth?" Gilly returned indignantly, poking Peter in his ribs. Peter laughed and the joking resumed, but not before Elizabeth witnessed the pain in her friend's expression.

An hour later, she helped Breed stow the sails after docking. Gilly and Peter carried the picnic basket and blankets to the car.

"Something's bothering Gilly," Elizabeth murmured to Breed the minute their friends were out of hearing distance.

"I noticed that, too," he whispered conspiratorially. "I think she's falling in love with Peter."

"No." She shook her head decisively. "They're just good friends."

"It may have started out like that, but it's not that way anymore." He sounded completely confident. He hardly paused as he moved forward to store the sails.

Elizabeth followed him. "What makes you so sure Gilly's in love?"

A weary look stole across his features. "She has that look about her." From his tone, she could tell he didn't want to discuss the subject further.

"Apparently you've seen that look in a lot of women's eyes," she stated teasingly, though with a serious undertone.

"A few," he responded noncommittally.

The thought of him loving another woman produced a curious ache in her heart. She paused and straightened. *So this is jealousy*, she mused. This churning sensation in the pit of her stomach, this inexplicable pain in her chest. As crazy as it seemed, she was jealous of some nameless other woman.

Breed's hand at her elbow brought her back to the present. He took her hand as he stepped onto the dock. "Peter and Gilly are waiting."

The silence coming from the back-seat of the car where Gilly and Peter were sitting was heavy and unnatural. A storm cloud seemed to have settled in the sedan, the air heavy with electricity. Breed captured Elizabeth's gaze and arched his brows in question.

She motioned weakly with her hand, telling him she had no more idea of what had happened between their friends than he did. Twice she attempted to start a conversation, but her words were met with uninterested grunts.

Breed pulled up and parked in front of the apartment she and Gilly shared. As he was helping Elizabeth, Gilly practically jumped from the car.

"Night, everyone," she said in a voice that was high-pitched and wobbly.

"Gilly, wait up. I want to talk to you." Peter bolted after her, his eyes filled with frustration. He cast Breed and Elizabeth an apologetic look on his way past.

Breed glanced at Elizabeth and

shrugged. "I'd say those two need some time alone."

"I agree."

"Do you want to go for a drive?" he suggested, tucking her hand under his folded arm as he led her back to the sedan.

"How about a walk instead? After sailing all evening, I could use some exercise."

He turned her in his arms. "We could. But I'd rather drive up to Coit Tower and show you the city lights. The view is fabulous."

Spending time alone with Breed was far more appealing than watching the city lights. "I'd like that," she admitted, getting back inside the car.

A long, winding drive through a dense neighborhood led to the observation tower situated high above the city. He parked, and as she stared out the windshield she realized that he hadn't exaggerated the view. She had seen some of the most beautiful landscapes in the world, but sitting with Breed overlooking San Francisco, she couldn't recall one more beautiful. Words couldn't describe the wonder of what lay before her.

"It's late," he murmured against her hair.

She acknowledged his words with a short nod, but she didn't want to leave and didn't suggest it.

"You have to work tomorrow." His voice was rough and soft, more of an aching whisper.

A smile touched her eyes. Breed couldn't decide if they should stay or go. Alone in the dark with nothing to distract them, the temptations were too great.

She tipped her head back. "Let me worry about tomorrow. I'll survive," she assured him. The night shaded his eyes, but she could feel the tension in him. His breathing was faintly irregular. "Why do you want to leave so much?" she asked in a throbbing whisper.

Her question went unanswered. A long moment of silence followed as he gazed down on her. Gently, he brushed the wispy strands of hair from her cheek, then curled his fingers into her hair. Elizabeth was shocked to realize he was trembling.

Slowly his head moved downward and paused an inch above her lips. "You know why we should leave," he growled.

All day she had yearned for him. Not for the first time, she noticed that he had been physically distant today, his touch casual, as though he was struggling to hold himself back. His restraint made her want him all the more.

"Beth." He whispered her name, and something snapped within him. His mouth plundered hers, and all her senses came to life. She rose slightly from the seat to press closer to him.

A tiny moan slipped from her as his lips found her neck and shot wave after wave of sensual delight through her. Her hands roamed his back, then moved forward and unfastened his shirt. Eagerly she let them glide down the smooth flat muscles of his broad chest.

He groaned and straightened, then buried his face in her neck and held her to him. "Beth…" he moaned. She could feel and see the conflict in his eyes.

He rubbed one hand across his face and eyes, but he continued to hold her tightly to him with the other, as though he couldn't bear to release her yet.

His control was almost frightening. The marvel of it silenced her for several seconds.

With her arms linked behind his head, she pressed her forehead to his.

The tension eased from his muscles, and she could hear the uneven thud of his heart slowly return to normal. When his breathing was less ragged, she lightly pressed her lips to his.

"Don't do that," he said harshly, abruptly releasing her. The tension in him was barely suppressed.

She turned away and leaned her head against the back of the seat, staring straight ahead. When tears of anger and frustration filled her eyes, she blinked hurriedly to forestall their flow.

"There's only so much of this a man can take." He, too, stared straight ahead as he savagely rubbed his hand along the back of his neck. "You know as well as I do what's happening between us."

"I can't help it, Breed," she whispered achingly.

"Yes, you can," he returned grimly.

The aching desire to reach across the close confines of the car and touch him was unbearable. But she didn't dare. She couldn't look at him. "Is…is there something wrong with me?" she asked in a tortured whisper. "I mean, do my freckles turn you off...or something?" Out of the corner of her eye, she saw a muscle twitch in his lean jaw.

"That question isn't worthy of an answer." His eyes hardened as he turned the ignition key and revved the engine.

"Maybe we should stop seeing so much of each other." Her pride was hurt, but the ache extended deep into her heart.

"Maybe we should," he said at last.

Elizabeth closed her eyes against the onrush of emotional pain. One tear escaped and made a wet track down her pale face, followed by another and another.

When he pulled up in front of her apartment building, she didn't turn to him to say good-night. She didn't want him to see her tears. That would only humiliate her further.

"Thanks for a lovely day," she whispered, barely able to find her voice; then she hurriedly opened the door and raced into the apartment foyer.

Breed didn't follow her, but he didn't leave either. His car was still parked outside when Elizabeth reached her apartment and, from deep within the living-room shadows, glanced out the window to watch him. The streetlight silhouetted a dejected figure of a man leaning over the steering wheel.

After a moment she realized that soft, whimpering cries were coming from the bedroom. Trapped in her own problems, she had forgotten Gilly's.

Wiping the moisture from her cheeks, she turned and headed down the hall to knock against her friend's open bedroom door.

"Gilly," she whispered, "what's wrong?"

Gilly sat up on her bed and blew noisily into a tissue. "Beth, I am so stupid."

"If you want to talk, I have all the time in the world to listen." She entered the darkened room and sat on the end of the bed. With all the problems she was having, she chastised herself for not recognizing what had been happening to her friend.

Gilly took another tissue and wiped her eyes dry. "Do you remember how I told you that Peter and I are just friends?"

"I remember."

"Well…" Gilly sniffled noisily, "something changed. I don't know when or why, but sometime last week I looked at Peter and I knew I loved him."

Elizabeth patted Gilly's hand. "That's no reason to cry. I'd think you'd be happy."

"I was, for two glorious days. I wanted to tell someone, but I didn't think it was fair to confide in you. I thought Peter should be the first one to know."

Her roommate *had* appeared exceptionally happy lately, Elizabeth recalled. Gilly had been particularly enthusiastic about the four of them spending the holiday together. She hadn't really thought much about it, though, because Gilly was always happy.

"Then I made the mistake of telling him," she continued. "You were helping Breed put the sails away, and Peter and I were carrying things to the car." She inhaled a quivering breath.

"What happened?" Elizabeth encouraged her roommate softly.

"I guess I should have waited for a more appropriate moment, but I was eager to talk to him. Everything about the day had been perfect, and we were alone for the first time. So, like an idiot, I turned to him and said, 'Peter, I don't know what's happened, but I love you.'"

"And?"

"First he looked shocked. Then embarrassed. He stuttered something about this being a surprise and looked like he wanted to run away, but then you and Breed returned and we all piled into the car."

"What happened when Breed dropped the two of you off here?"

"Nothing. I wouldn't talk to him."

"Gilly!"

"You wouldn't have wanted to talk, either," she insisted, defending her actions. "I was humiliated enough without Peter apologizing to me because he didn't share my feelings."

"I'm sure he's going to want to talk to you." Elizabeth appealed to the more reasonable part of her friend's nature.

"He can forget it. How could I have been so stupid? If I was going to fall in love, why couldn't it be with someone like Breed?"

Elizabeth lowered her gaze to her hands. "There's only one Breed, and he's mine."

"Oh, before I forget..." Gilly sat up and looked around her, finally handing

Elizabeth a piece of paper with a phone number written across the top. "Your brother phoned."

"My brother? From Boston?"

"No, he's here in San Francisco. He's staying at the Saint Francis. I told him I didn't know what time you'd be back, so he said to tell you that he'd expect you tomorrow night for dinner at seven-thirty at his hotel."

Ordering instead of asking. That sounded just like her brother.

"Did he say anything else?" It would be just like Charlie to say something to embarrass her.

Gilly shook her head. "Not really, except..."

"Yes?" Elizabeth stiffened.

"Well, your brother's not like you, is he?"

"How do you mean?" Elizabeth asked.

"I don't know, exactly. But after I hung

up, I wondered if I should have curtsied or something."

After a single telephone conversation, the astute Gilly had her brother pegged. "He's like that," Elizabeth admitted.

"Well, anyway, I gave you the message."

"And I'll show up at the hotel and hope I use the right spoon or my dear brother will be outraged."

For the first time that evening, Gilly smiled.

The café hadn't been open for more than five minutes when Breed strolled in and sat at his regular table. Elizabeth caught sight of his broad shoulders the moment he entered. Even after all these weeks her heart stirred at the sight of him, and now it throbbed painfully. One part of her wanted to rush to him, but she resisted.

Carrying the coffeepot, she approached

his table slowly. He turned over the ceramic mug for her.

"Morning," she said as unemotionally as possible.

"Morning," he echoed.

Her eyes refused to meet his, but she could feel his gaze concentrating on her. "Would you like a menu?"

"No, just coffee."

She filled his cup.

"We need to talk," he announced casually as his hands folded around the cup.

She blinked uncertainly. "I can't now," she replied nervously. "Mornings are our busiest time."

"I didn't mean now." The words were enunciated slowly, as if his control over his patience had been stretched to the limit. "Tonight would be better, when we're able to discuss things freely, don't you think?"

She shifted her weight from one foot to the other. "I can't," she murmured apologetically. "My brother's in town, and I'm meeting him for dinner."

His level gaze darted to her, his eyes disbelieving.

"It's true," she declared righteously. "We're meeting at the Saint Francis."

"I believe you."

Frustrated, she watched as a hard mask stole over his face. "Go have dinner with your brother, then."

"I wasn't waiting for your approval," Elizabeth remarked angrily.

His amber eyes blazed for a furious second. "I didn't think you were."

Indecision made her hesitate. She wanted to turn and give him a clear view of her back, yet at the same time she wanted to set things right between them. The harmony they'd shared so often over these past weeks was slowly disintegrating before her eyes.

"Would you care to join us?" The question slipped from her naturally, although her mind was screaming for him to refuse.

"Me?" He looked aghast. "You don't mean that."

"I wouldn't have asked you otherwise." What, she wondered, had she been thinking? The entire evening would be a disaster. She could just imagine Charlie's reaction to someone like Breed.

Breed appeared to give her invitation some consideration. "No," he said at last, and she couldn't prevent the low but controlled breath of relief. "Maybe another time."

"Do you want to meet later?" she asked, and her voice thinned to a quavering note. "Dinner shouldn't take long," she said, glancing down at her practical white shoes. "I want to talk to you, too."

"Not tonight." The lines bracketing his mouth deepened with his growing impatience. Although she'd asked him to join her and Charlie, she realized that he knew she didn't want him there. "I'll give you a call later in the week." He stood, and with determined strides left the café.

She watched him go and had the irrational urge to throw his untouched coffee after him. That arrogant male pride of his only fueled her anger.

That night Elizabeth dressed carefully in a raspberry-colored dress with a delicate white miniprint. A dress that would meet with Charlie's approval, she mused as she examined herself in the mirror. Not until it was time to go did she stop to consider why he was in town. The family had no business holdings on the West Coast. At least none that she knew about. She hoped he hadn't come to persuade her to return to Boston. She'd just about made up her mind to make San Francisco her permanent home. The city was lovely, and the thought of leaving

Breed was intolerable. She wouldn't—couldn't—leave the man she loved.

The taxi delivered her to the entrance of the prestigious hotel at precisely seven-twenty. The extra minutes gave her the necessary time to compose herself. She was determined to make this a pleasant evening. A confrontation with her brother was the last thing she wanted.

"Lizzy."

She groaned inwardly. Only one person in the world called her that.

"Hello, Siggy." She forced herself to smile and extended her hand for him to shake. To her acute embarrassment, he pulled her into his arms and kissed her soundly. Her mouth was opened in surprise, and Siggy seemed to assume she was eager for his attention and deepened the kiss.

Without making a scene, Elizabeth was left to endure his despicable touch.

The sound of someone clearing his

throat appeared to bring Siggy back to his senses. He broke the contact, and it was all Elizabeth could do not to rub the feel of his mouth from hers with the back of her hand. His touch made her skin crawl, and she glared angrily from him to her brother.

"There are better places for such an intimate greeting," Charlie said, slapping Siggy on the back. "I told you she'd be happy to see you."

Siggy ignored Charlie and said, "It's good to see you, Lizzy."

She was unable to restrain her involuntary grimace. "Don't call me Lizzy," she said between clenched teeth.

Charlie glanced at his slim gold watch. "Our table should be ready. Names are something I'll leave for you two to discuss later."

Later. She cringed at the thought. There wasn't going to be a later with Siggy, though at least now she under-

stood why Charlie had come to San Francisco. He wanted to foist Siggy on her.
She hadn't thought about it at the time,
but Charlie had mentioned Siggy at every
opportunity lately. That was the reason
she'd found herself avoiding her brother,
who stood to benefit from any marriage
between the two families. His selfishness
made her want to cry.

By some miracle she was able to endure the meal. She spoke only when a
question was directed to her and smiled
politely at appropriate intervals. The
knot in her throat extended all the way
to her abdomen and felt like a rock in
the pit of her stomach. The two men discussed her at length, commenting several
times on how good she looked. Charlie
insisted that she would make a radiant
bride and declared that their father would
be proud of her, knowing she had chosen
so well. He made marriage between her
and Siggy sound like a foregone conclu-

sion. Questions buzzed around her head like irritating bees. In the past she'd had her differences with her father, but he wouldn't do this to her. She had to believe that. Yet her father *had* mentioned Siggy during their last few telephone conversations.

Resignedly, she accompanied her brother and Siggy to Charlie's suite for an after-dinner drink.

The small glass of liqueur helped chase the chill from her slender frame. Siggy sat on the plush sofa beside her and draped his arm possessively around her shoulders. She found his touch suffocating and pointedly removed his arm, then scooted to the other end of the sofa. Undaunted, he followed.

"I can see that you two have a lot to discuss," Charlie said, exchanging knowing smiles with the younger man. Without another word, he excused himself and left Elizabeth alone to deal with

Siggy. The moment the door clicked closed, Siggy was on her like a starving man after food.

Pinned against the corner of the couch, she jerked her head left and right in an effort to avoid his punishing kiss.

"Siggy!" she gasped, pushing him off her. "Stop it!"

Composing himself, Siggy sat upright and made a pretense of straightening his tie. "I'm sorry, Lizzy. It's just that I love you so much. I've wanted you for years, and now I know you feel the same way."

"What?" she exploded.

Siggy brushed a stray hair from her flushed cheek. "Charlie told me how you've had a crush on me for years. Why didn't you say something? You must have known how I feel about you. I've never made any secret of that."

A lump of outrage and shocked disbelief grew in her. Charlie had selfishly and maliciously lied to Siggy. Her own brother had sold her for thirty pieces of silver. She was nothing more to Charlie than the means of securing a financial coup that would link two wealthy families.

"Where is my brother?" Elizabeth managed finally. "I'd like to talk to him."

"He'll be back," Siggy said, as he stood, crossed the room and helped himself to another glass of brandy. "He wanted to give us some time alone. Want some, darling?" He held up the brandy and eyed her solicitously.

"No." Irritated, she shook her head. "So what would happen to the two companies if our families were linked?"

Smug and secure, Siggy silently toasted her. "A merger. It will be the financial feat of the year, Charlie says. My family will give him the exclusive distribution contract for our stores. Already we're planning to expand within a three-state area."

Momentarily shocked, Elizabeth felt tears form in her eyes. It was little wonder that Charlie was doing this. A lucrative—and exclusive—contract with Siggy's family's chain of department stores was something the Wainwrights had sought for years. But the price was far too high. Her happiness was not a bargaining chip.

Charlie returned a few minutes later, looking pleased and excited.

"If you'll excuse us a minute, Siggy," Elizabeth said bluntly, "I'd like to talk to my brother. Alone."

"Sure." Siggy glanced from brother to sister before setting his drink aside. "I'll be in the lounge when you're finished."

The second the door clicked closed, Elizabeth whirled on her brother. "How could you?" she demanded.

Charlie knotted his fists at his sides. "Listen, little sister, you're not going to ruin this for me. Not this time."

"Charlie, I'm your only sister. How could you ask me to marry a man I don't love? A man I don't even respect…"

His mouth tightened grimly. "For once in your life, stop thinking of yourself."

"Me?"

"Yes, you." He paced the floor in short, angry strides. "All right, I admit I went about this poorly, but marrying Siggy is what Mother would have wanted for you."

"That's not true." Her mother knew her feelings about Siggy and would never have pressured her into something like this.

"What do you know?" He hurled the words at her furiously. "You only thought of yourself. You never knew what Mother was really thinking. It was your selfishness that killed her."

The blood drained from Elizabeth's face. She and her mother had spent the afternoon shopping, and when they got back her mother, who wasn't feeling well, had gone to lie down before dinner. Within an hour she was dead, the victim of a massive stroke. In the back of her mind, she had always carried the guilt that something she had done that day had caused her death.

"Charlie, please," she whispered frantically. "Don't say that. Please don't say that."

"But it's true!" he shouted. "I was with father when the doctor said that having you drag her from store to store was simply too much. It killed her. *You* killed her."

"Oh, dear God." She felt her knees buckle as she slumped onto the sofa.

"There's only one thing you can do now to make up for that, Elizabeth. Do what Mother would have wanted. Marry Siggy. It would have made her happy."

He was lying. In her soul, she knew he was lying. But her own flesh and blood, her only brother, whom she had loved and adored in her youth, had used the cruellest weapon in his arsenal against her. With hot tears scalding her cheeks, she stood, clenched her purse to her breast and walked out the door.

She didn't stop walking until she found a taxi. Between breathless but controlled sobs, she gave the cabbie her address. Not until he pulled away from the curb did she realize how badly she was shaking.

"Are you all right, lady?" The cabbie looked at her anxiously in the rearview mirror.

She couldn't manage anything more than a nod.

When they arrived in front of her apartment, she handed him a twenty-dollar bill and didn't wait for the change. Though she had calmed down slightly on the ride home, she didn't want Gilly to see her, so she hurried in the door and headed for her bedroom.

"You're back soon." The sound of the television drifted from the living room.

"Yes," Elizabeth mumbled, keeping her head lowered, not wanting her friend to see her tears. She continued walking. "I think I'll take a bath and go to bed."

Gilly must have looked up for the first time. The sound of her surprised gasp was like an assault, and Elizabeth flinched. "Elizabeth! Good grief, what's wrong?"

"Nothing." Elizabeth looked at the wall. "I'm fine. I just need to be alone." She went into the bedroom and closed the door, leaning against it. Reaction set in, and she started to shake uncontrollably again. Fresh tears followed. Tears of anger. Tears of hate. Tears of pain and pride.

Softly Gilly knocked on the closed bedroom door, but Elizabeth ignored her.

She didn't want to explain. She couldn't, not when she was crying like this. She fell into bed and curled up in a tight ball in an attempt to control the freezing cold that made her shake so violently.

When she inhaled between sobs, she heard Gilly talking to someone. Her friend's voice was slightly high-pitched and worried. She felt guilty that she was worrying Gilly like this, but she couldn't help it. Later she would make up some excuse. But she couldn't now.

Five minutes later there was another knock on her door. Elizabeth ignored it.

"Beth," a male voice said softly. "Open up. It's me."

"Breed," she sobbed, throwing back the covers. "Oh, Breed." She opened the door and fell into his arms, weeping uncontrollably. Every part of her clung to him as he lifted her into his arms and carried her into the living room.

With an infinite gentleness he set her

on the couch and brushed the hair from her face.

One look at her and he stiffened. "Who did this to you?"

Seven

Elizabeth was crying so hard that she couldn't answer. Nor did she know how to explain. She didn't want to tell Breed and Gilly that the brother she loved had betrayed her in the worst possible way.

Breed said something to Gilly, but Elizabeth didn't hear. "Beth," he whispered, leading her to the couch and half lifting her onto his lap. "Tell me what's upset you."

Forcefully, she shook her head and inhaled deep breaths that became quivering sobs as she tried to regain control of herself. Crying like this was only making matters worse.

She knew the terrible, crippling pain of Charlie's betrayal was there in her eyes, and she couldn't do anything to conceal it. A nerve twitched in Breed's hard, lean jaw, his features tense, and pain showed clearly in his eyes. *Her* pain. She was suffering, and that caused him to hurt as well. She couldn't have loved anyone more than she loved him right at that moment. She didn't know what he thought had happened, and she couldn't utter a word to assure him.

"I'm fine. No one hurt me...not physically," she finally said in a trembling voice she barely recognized as her own. "Just hold me." She had trouble trying to control her breathing. Her body continued to shake with every inhalation.

"I'll never let you go," he promised as his lips moved against her hair. She felt some of the tension leave him, felt his relief that things weren't as bad as he'd thought.

Warm blankets were wrapped around her, so warm they must have recently been taken from the dryer. That must be what Breed had asked Gilly to do, Elizabeth realized.

He continued to talk to her in a low, soothing tone until her eyes drifted closed. Caught between sleep and reality, she could feel him gently free himself from her embrace and lay her on the sofa. A pillow cushioned her head, and warm blankets surrounded her. She didn't know how long he knelt beside her, smoothing her hair from her face, his touch so tender she felt secure and protected. Gradually a calmness filled her, and she knew she was on the brink of falling asleep. Breed left her side but she sensed that he hadn't gone far. He had told her he wouldn't leave, and she was comforted just by knowing he was in the same room.

"All I know," Elizabeth heard Gilly whisper, "was that she was meeting her brother for dinner. What could he have done to cause this?"

"You can bet I'm going to find out," Breed stated in a dry, hard voice that was frightening in its intensity.

"No." Elizabeth struggled to a sitting position. "Just drop the whole thing. It's my own affair."

Breed's eyes narrowed.

"Elizabeth," Gilly murmured, her eyes wide and worried, "I've never seen you like this."

"I'm fine, really." She brushed back her tear-dampened hair. "I'm just upset. I apologize for making a scene."

"You didn't make a scene," Gilly returned soothingly.

Breed brought her a damp cloth and, kneeling at her side, gently brushed it over her cheeks. It felt cool and soothing over her hot skin. His jaw was clenched and pale, as if he couldn't stand to have her hurt in any way, physically or emotionally.

Elizabeth stroked the side of his face, then pulled him to her, wrapping her arms around his neck. "Thank you."

"For what? I should have been there for you."

"You couldn't have known." It wasn't right that he should shoulder any blame for what had happened.

He took her hands and gently raised them to his mouth, then kissed her knuckles. "Beth…" His eyes implored hers. "I want you to trust me enough to tell me what happened tonight."

She lowered her gaze and shook her head. "It's done. I don't want to go over it."

The pressure on her fingers was punishing for a quick second. "I'll kill anyone who hurts you like this again."

"That's exactly why I won't talk about it."

The tension between them was so palpable that she could taste it. Their eyes clashed in a test of wills. Unnerved, she lowered hers first. "I need you here," she whispered in a soft plea. "It's over now. I want to forget it ever happened."

Gilly hovered close. "Do you feel like you could drink something? Tea? Coffee? Soda?"

The effort to smile was painful. "All I want is a hot bath and bed." Her muscles ached, and she discovered that when she stood, her legs wobbled unsteadily, so she leaned against Breed for a moment.

Gilly hurried ahead and filled the bathtub with steaming, scented water. Next she brought in fluffy, fresh towels.

"You want me to stay in the bathroom while you soak?" Breed asked, and a crooked smile slanted his mouth, because of course he knew the answer. The humor didn't quite touch his eyes, but Elizabeth appreciated the effort.

"No. If I need anyone, Gilly can help."

"Pity," he grumbled.

The hot water helped relieve the aching tension in her muscles. Even now her body was coiled and alert. The throbbing in her temples diminished, and the pain in her heart began to recede. As she rested against the back of the tub, she kept running over the details of the evening, but she forced the painful images to the back of her mind. She didn't feel strong enough emotionally to deal with things now. Maybe tomorrow.

Gilly stayed with her, more on Breed's insistence than because she felt Elizabeth needed her. Together they emerged from the steam-filled bathroom, Elizabeth wrapped in her thick terry robe. Breed led Elizabeth into her room. The sheets on her bed had been folded back, and her weak smile silently thanked him.

"You won't leave me?" Her eyes pleaded with him as he tucked her under the covers.

"No," he whispered. "I said I wouldn't." His kiss was so tender that fresh tears misted her eyes. "Go to sleep," he whispered encouragingly.

"You'll be here when I wake up?" She needed that reassurance.

"I'll be here."

The dark void was already pulling her into its welcoming arms. As she drifted into sleep, she could hear Breed's low voice quizzing Gilly.

The sound of someone obviously trying to be quiet and not succeeding woke Elizabeth. The room was dark, and she glanced at her clock radio to note that it was just after three. She sat up in bed and blinked. The memory of the events of the evening pressed heavily against her heart. Although she was confident Charlie would never have abandoned her to Siggy if her brother had known what Siggy was capable of doing, the sense of betrayal remained. To try to push her off on Siggy was deplorable enough. Slipping from between the sheets, she put on her silk housecoat and moved into the living room.

"Hello there," she whispered to Breed, keeping quiet so she wouldn't disrupt Gilly's sleep.

"Did I wake you?" He sat up and wiped a hand across his weary face. The sight of him trying to sleep on the couch was ludicrous. His feet dangled far over the end, and he looked all elbows and arms.

"You wake me? Never. I thought an elephant had escaped and was raging through the living room."

His smile was evident in the moonlight. "I got up to use the bathroom and walked into the lamp," he explained with a chagrined look.

"It was selfish of me to ask you to stay," she said, sitting down beside him.

"I would have stayed whether you asked me to or not." He reached for her hand and squeezed it gently. "How do you feel?"

She shrugged and lowered her gaze to her knees. "Like a fool. I don't usually overreact that way."

"I know," he murmured. "That's what concerned me most." He put his arm around her, and she rested her head against his shoulder. "Sometimes the emotional pain can be twice as bad as anything physical." She gave a long, drawn-out yawn. "When you love and trust someone and they hurt you, then the pain goes beyond anything physical." She began explaining the situation to Breed, though carefully tiptoeing around any discussion of her family's wealth. He'd asked her to trust him, and she did, at least with her feelings. It was important that he realize that.

He didn't comment, but she felt him stiffen slightly. When she leaned against his solid support, he pulled her close, holding her to his chest.

Soon the comfort of his arms lured her back to sleep. When she woke again, she discovered that they had both fallen asleep while sitting upright. His arm was still draped around her, and he rested his head against the back of the sofa. His breathing was deep and undisturbed.

Even from a sitting position, waking up in Breed's arms felt right. She pressed her face against the side of his neck and kissed him, enjoying the light taste of salt and musk.

"Are you pretending to be Sleeping Beauty kissing the handsome prince to wake him?" he asked, opening one eye to study her.

She barely allowed his sideways glance to touch her before straightening. "You've got that tale confused. It was the prince who kissed Sleeping Beauty awake."

"Would it hurt you if I did?" The teasing left his voice as he brought her closer within the protective circle of his arms.

Her eyes sought his. "You could never hurt me," she said in a whisper that sounded as solemn as a vow.

"I don't ever want to," he murmured as his lips claimed hers. The kiss was gentle and sweet. His mouth barely touched hers, enhancing the sensuality of the contact. His hands framed her face, and he treated her as if he were handling a rare and exotic orchid.

"You're looking much more chipper this morning," Gilly said, standing in the doorway of her bedroom. She raised her hands high above her head and yawned.

"I feel a whole lot better."

"I'm happy to hear that. I don't mind telling you that you had me worried."

"You?" Breed inhaled harshly. "I don't think I've ever come closer to wanting to kill a man. It's a good thing you didn't tell who did this last night, Beth. I wouldn't have been responsible for my actions."

Elizabeth lowered her gaze to the hands folded primly in her lap. "I think I already knew that."

"Take the day off," Gilly insisted as she sauntered into the kitchen and started the coffee.

"I can't do that," Elizabeth objected strenuously. "You need me."

"I'll make do," Gilly returned confidently. She opened the refrigerator, took out a pitcher of orange juice and poured herself a small glass. "But only for today."

Elizabeth returned to her bedroom to

change clothes. When she studied herself in the mirror she saw no outward mark of what she'd been through, but the mirror couldn't reveal the inner agony of what Charlie had tried to do.

"I don't believe it," she grumbled as she walked into the living room. "Last night I wanted to die, and today I feel like the luckiest woman alive to have you two as my friends."

"We're the lucky ones," Gilly said sincerely.

"But I acted like such a fool. I can't imagine what you thought."

"You were shocked, upset," Breed insisted with a note of confidence. "Shock often exaggerates the messages transmitted to the brain."

"Such a know-it-all," Gilly complained, running a brush through her short, bouncy curls. She looked at Elizabeth with a mischievous gleam. "Why do you put up with him?"

Elizabeth shrugged and shook her head. "I don't know. But he's kinda cute."

"I amuse you, is that it?" Breed joined in the teasing banter.

"You're amusing, but not always correct," Elizabeth remarked jokingly. "My brain wasn't confused by shock. But I'll admit, you had me going there for a minute."

He had the grace to look faintly embarrassed. "Well, it sounded good at the time."

Gilly paused on her way out the door. "Have a good day, you two. Call if you need anything. And—" she hesitated and lowered her gaze "—don't hold up dinner for me."

"Working late?" Elizabeth quizzed, experiencing a twinge of guilt that her friend would be stuck at the café alone.

Gilly shook her head. "Peter said he'd be coming by, and I don't want to be here when he does."

"Honestly, Gilly, you're acting like a child."

"Maybe." Gilly admitted. "But at least I've got my pride."

Breed murmured something about pride doing little to keep her warm at night, but luckily Gilly was too far away to hear him.

The door clicked, indicating Gilly had left for work.

"Are you hungry?" Breed asked as he walked across the living room, his hands buried deep inside his pants pockets.

She hadn't eaten much of her dinner the previous night, but even so, she discovered she didn't have much of an appetite. "Not really."

"What you need is something scintillating to tempt you."

Wickedly batting her eyelashes, she glanced at him and softly said, "My dear Mr. Breed, what exactly do you have in mind?"

He chose to ignore the comment.

"I think I'll go over to my place to shower and change. When I come back, I'll bring us breakfast."

Her mouth dropped in mute surprise. She couldn't believe he hadn't risen to her bait, and, selfishly, she didn't want him to leave her alone. Not now. "I'll come with you," she suggested eagerly. "And while you're in the shower, I'll cook us breakfast."

His expression revealed his lack of enthusiasm for her suggestion. "Not this time."

She bristled. "Why not?" The memory of her last visit to his apartment remained vivid. She hadn't been imagining things. He really didn't want her there. And yet she couldn't imagine why.

"You need to stay here and rest."

Her eyes widened in bewildered protest.

"I was thinking that while I'm gone you can get an extra hour's sleep."

Sleep? She was dressed and had downed a cup of strong coffee. He didn't honestly expect her to go back to bed, did he?

"I won't be long," he told her, and without a backward glance he hurried out the door.

"Don't worry about breakfast. I'll have something ready when you come back," she called after him. She didn't like this situation, but there wasn't much she could do. The impulse to speak her mind died on her lips. Now wasn't the time to confront Breed with petty suspicions about her cool welcome at his apartment.

With a cookbook resting on the kitchen counter, she skimmed over the recipe for blueberry muffins. For the moment, keeping busy was paramount. When she stopped to think, too many dark images crowded her thoughts. For a time last night she had started to believe Charlie's vindictive words, which fed on the fear that she was somehow responsible for her mother's death, which had haunted her ever since that awful day. When a tear escaped, despite her determination not to cry, she wiped it aside angrily and forced herself to concentrate on the recipe. Rehashing the details of last night only upset her, so she soundly rejected any more introspection on the subject.

As promised, Breed returned less than an hour later.

A hand on each of her shoulders, he kissed her lightly on the cheek. He looked wonderful, his hair still wet from his shower.

"Hmm…something smells good."

"I baked some muffins," she said as she led the way into the kitchen. Her culinary efforts were cooling on a rack on top of the counter. "I don't know how they taste. The cookbook said they were great to take camping."

"Are you thinking of taking me into the woods and ravaging my body?" he joked as he lifted a muffin from the cooling rack. It burned his fingers, and he gingerly tossed it in the air several times until, laughing, she handed him a plate.

"You might have told me they were still hot."

"And miss seeing you juggle? Never." Her mood had lightened to match his. Sitting beside him at the circular table, she peeled an orange and popped a section into her mouth.

"How about a trip to our beach today?" he suggested, and his mouth curved into a sensuous smile.

"Sure." Her glance caught sight of his massive hands. A slight swelling in one of the knuckles captured her attention. Had he been fighting? Showering wouldn't have taken him an hour. Immediately the thought flashed through her mind that he'd gone to see her brother. "Breed…" Her eyes sought his as she swallowed past the thickness lodged in her throat. "Give me your hand."

The teasing glitter didn't leave his eyes, and he didn't seem to notice the serious light in hers. "Is this a proposal of marriage?"

"Let me see your hand," she repeated.

He went completely still. "Why?"

"Because I need to know that you didn't do anything…dumb."

He smiled briefly and pushed his chair away from the table, then stood and walked to the other side of the room, folding his arms across his massive chest. Expelling an explosive breath, he replied, "I didn't, although the temptation was strong. While I live, no man will ever treat you that way again."

"I appreciate the chivalry," she said evenly, "but I wish you hadn't."

"I found it...necessary." The hard set of his features revealed the tight hold he was keeping on both his temper and his emotions.

Her composure cracked. "I'm not defending him...."

"I should hope not." He shook his head grimly.

"But I don't want you involved," she said.

"I'm already involved."

She stood and, with her own arms folded around her narrow waist, paced the kitchen. The room was filled with Breed. His presence loomed in every corner. "Please understand, I don't want to argue with you."

His eyes narrowed as he moved into the other room and sat on the arm of the sofa. "I've never met anyone like you, Beth. Those two deserve to have the stuffing kicked out of them."

"He's my brother!" she cried defensively. "He may not be a very nice guy, but he's the only one I've got."

He moved into the living room, his back to her. When he turned to face her again a moment later, his grim look had vanished. "Are we going to the beach or not?"

Numbly, she nodded.

"Good." With long strides he crossed the distance separating them. Then he took her by the shoulders and sweetly kissed her. "Let's hurry. It's isn't every day that I get you all to myself."

They rode in his silver sedan, and again she wondered why he no longer drove Hilda. Maybe the Jeep needed repairs and he couldn't afford to have them done until his finances improved. She wished there was some way she could take care of things like that for him without his knowing. Offering him money wasn't the answer, only a sure way of crushing his male ego. Even so, what was the use of having money if she couldn't spend it the way she wanted?

The surf rolled gently against their bare feet as they strolled along the smooth beach, their arms entwined.

"Tell my about your childhood," he asked curiously after a lengthy, companionable silence.

Under other circumstances she might have had the courage to reveal her wealth. But not today. She'd faced enough upheaval in the last twenty-four hours to warrant caution. Her mouth tightened with tension before she managed to speak.

"What's there to tell? I was born, grew up, went to school, graduated, went to school some more, dropped out, and traveled a little."

"Nicely condensed, I'd say."

"Have you been to Europe?" she asked, to change the subject.

"No, but I spent six months in New

Zealand a few years back." His response told her he knew exactly what she was doing.

"Did you enjoy it?" Relieved, she continued the game.

"I'd say it was the most beautiful country on earth, but I haven't done enough traveling to compare it with the rest of the world."

She recalled her own trip to the South Pacific. Her time in New Zealand had been short, but she'd shared his feelings about the island nation.

"My mother used to love to travel," she commented, mentally recalling the many trips they'd taken together.

"How long has she been gone?" he asked, his hand reaching for hers.

She swallowed with difficulty and forced her chin up in a defensive stance. "She died two years ago," she explained softly. "Even after all this time, I miss her."

He paused, and traced a finger over her jaw and down her neck. "I'm sorry, Beth. You must have loved her very much."

"I did," she whispered on a weak note.

"Did your family ever go camping?" The question came out of the blue and was obviously meant to change the mood.

"No." She had never slept in a tent in her life. Back-to-nature pursuits had never been among her father's interests.

"Would you like to sometime?"

"Us?"

"I was thinking of inviting Gilly along." Gently, his hand closed over hers. "And Peter," he added as an afterthought.

"Peter? You devious little devil."

"Of course, that will take some finagling," he admitted.

"Finagling or downright deception?"

"Deception," he immediately agreed.

"You shock me, Andrew Breed. I

wouldn't have guessed that you had a sneaky bone in your body."

His gaze slid past her to the rolling waves that broke against the sand. "I suspect a lot of things about me would shock you," he murmured, and her thoughts echoed his.

"What really irritates me," Gilly continued her tirade as she hauled another box of cooking utensils out from the kitchen, "is the fact that I bare my heart to Peter and then he—he just disappears. It's been three days since I've heard from him. Count 'em, Beth, three long days."

"Well, you slammed the door in his face last time he came over, and you hang up on him whenever he calls."

"Well, he deserves it."

Hands on hips, Gilly surveyed the living-room floor. Half of the contents of their kitchen had been packed into cardboard boxes in anticipation of the week-end camping trip. "Is that everything?"

"Well, I certainly hope so." Elizabeth couldn't believe that people actually went through all this work just for a couple of days of traipsing around the woods.

When Breed arrived he looked incredulously at the accumulated gear.

"Before you complain, I only packed what was on your list," Elizabeth said as she flashed him an eager smile. She was ready for this new adventure, although she was suffering a few qualms about not telling Gilly that Peter had been invited. In fact, he had left the night before and claimed a space for them in the Samuel P. Taylor State Park, north of the city.

"Well, maybe we packed a few things not on your meager list," Gilly amended. "You left off several things we might need."

"I don't know how Hilda's going to

carry all this," Breed mumbled under his breath.

"Hilda," Elizabeth cried happily. "We're taking Hilda?" Before Breed could stop her, she rushed down the stairs to the outdated Jeep parked at the curb. Gingerly she climbed into the front seat and patted the dashboard. "It's good to see you again," she murmured affectionately.

"Will someone kindly tell me what's going on?" Gilly stood, one hand placed on her hip, staring curiously at her friend.

"It's a long story," Breed murmured, lifting the first box on board.

Admittedly it was a tight squeeze, but they managed to fit everything.

The radio blared, and they were all singing along as they traveled. When the news came on, they paused to listen. From her squashed position in the backseat, Gilly leaned forward. "Hey, Breed, I don't see any tent back here."

"There isn't one," he said with a smile, glancing at Elizabeth.

"I thought we were going camping?"

"We are," he confirmed.

"With no tent?"

Elizabeth didn't want to carry the deception any further. "Peter pitched the tent yesterday."

"Peter!" Gilly exploded. "You didn't say anything about Peter coming on this trip."

Elizabeth turned and faced her friend. "Are you mad?"

Gilly's gaze raked Elizabeth's worried face. Folding her arms, she resolutely stared out the window. "Why should I be mad? My best friend in the world has just turned traitor."

"If I'm your best friend, then you have to believe I wouldn't do anything to hurt you," Elizabeth returned with quiet logic.

"I'm not answering that."

"Because I'm right," Elizabeth argued irrefutably.

"Peter loves you," Breed inserted, matching Gilly's clipped tones. "And if it means kidnapping you so that he has the chance to explain himself, then I don't consider that much of a crime."

"I suppose you think that someday I'll thank you for this."

"I want to be maid of honor," Elizabeth said with a romantic sigh.

Gilly ignored her and sat in stony silence until Breed turned off the highway and entered the campgrounds. Peter had left word of his location at the ranger station, and within a matter of minutes they were at the campsite.

"I hope you realize that I don't appreciate this one bit," Gilly said through clenched teeth.

"I believe we got the picture." Breed's mouth curved in a humorous smile.

"Really, Gilly, it won't be so bad. All

we want is for you to give the poor guy a chance."

Gilly ignored her friend and turned her attention to Breed. "Did you know Beth once called you Tarzan?" she informed him saucily.

"Tarzan?" Breed's large eyes rounded indignantly, and he turned to Elizabeth with a feigned look of outrage. "Beth, you didn't."

She forced herself to smile and nodded regretfully.

"In that case, will you be my Jane?"

"Love to," she returned happily, placing her hand in his.

Peter had the tent pitched and a small fire going when they arrived. Breed and Elizabeth climbed out of the front seat and stretched. Gilly remained inside, her arms folded as she stared defiantly ahead.

"Hi, Gilly," Peter said as he strolled

up to the Jeep, his hands buried in his pockets.

Silence.

Peter continued, "I've always been one to lay my cards on the table, so you're going to listen to me. There's no place to run now."

More silence.

He went on, "You once told me that you loved me, but I'm beginning to have my doubts about that." He levered himself so that he was in the driver's seat and turned to face her. "I was so shocked at your announcement that I must have said and done the worst possible things." He hesitated slightly. "The thing was, I had no idea how you felt."

"Your reaction told me that." Gilly spoke for the first time, her words tight and low.

"You see, I'd realized earlier how much you'd come to mean to me. I'd been trying to work up enough nerve to tell you my feelings had changed."

"Don't you dare lie to me, Peter."

"I'm not," he returned harshly. "For too long I've had doors shut in my face, phones slammed in my ear. I've about had it, Gillian Haggith. I want you to marry me, and I want your answer right now."

Feeling like an intruder, Elizabeth leaned against the picnic table with Breed at her side. Fascinated, she watched as Gilly's mouth opened and closed incredulously. For the first time in recent history, her friend was utterly speechless.

"Maybe this will help you decide," Peter mumbled, withdrawing a small diamond ring from his jeans pocket.

"Oh, Peter!" Gilly cried, and she threw her arms around him as she burst into happy tears.

Eight

"Shall we give the lovebirds some time alone?" Breed whispered in Elizabeth's ear.

Her nod was indulgent. "How about giving me a grand tour of the grounds."

"Love to."

"I'm especially interested in the modern technological advances."

His thoughtful gaze swept over her face. "Beth, we're in the woods. There are no technological wonders out here."

"I was thinking of things that go flush in the night."

"Ahh, those." The corners of his mouth twitched briefly upward. "Allow me to lead the way."

He set a comfortable pace as they wandered around the campgrounds, taking their time. The sky couldn't have been any bluer, and the air was filled with the scent of pine and evergreen. A creek bubbled cheerfully down its meandering course, and they paused for a few quiet moments of peaceful introspection. Elizabeth's thoughts drifted to her father. Their showcase home in Boston, with all its splendor, couldn't compare to the tranquil beauty of this forest. If he could see this place, she was confident, he would experience the serenity that had touched her in so brief a time.

Gilly had lunch cooking by the time Breed and Elizabeth returned. The two of them smiled conspiratorially, having agreed to pretend ignorance of the conversation they'd overheard earlier. With an efficiency Elizabeth hardly recognized in her friend, Gilly set out the paper plates, a pan of hot beans, freshly made potato salad, and grilled hot dogs with toasted buns.

"I'll do the dishes," Elizabeth joked as she filled her paper plate. Gilly sat beside Elizabeth at the picnic table.

"I'm sorry about what I said earlier," Gilly murmured as telltale color crept up her neck. "It was childish and immature of me to tell Breed that you once referred to him as Tarzan." She released her breath with a thin edge of exasperation. "Actually, it was probably the stupidest thing I've ever done in my entire life. How petty can I get?"

"You had a right to be angry." Even so, Elizabeth appreciated her friend's apology. "Not telling you that Peter was coming here was underhanded and conniving."

Breed lifted his index finger. "And my idea. I take credit."

Elizabeth's eyes captured his, and her gaze wavered slightly under his potent spell. "But if it had backfired, the blame would have been mine. I'm learning a lot about the workings of the male mind."

"Do you have to sit across the table from me, woman?" Peter complained as he settled next to Breed.

"I'll be sitting next to you for the rest of my life," Gilly returned with a happy note. "Besides, at this angle you can feast upon my unspoiled beauty."

The diamond ring on her finger sparkled almost as brightly as the happiness in her eyes. Things couldn't have worked out better. Elizabeth realized how miserable her friend had been the last few days and felt oddly guilty that she had been so involved in her own problems.

"Do you two have an announcement to

make?" Breed asked as he stared pointedly at Gilly's left hand.

"Gilly and I are getting married," Peter informed them cheerfully.

"We haven't set a date yet," Gilly inserted. "Peter thought we should talk to my parents first. And my church has a counseling class for engaged couples. I thought we should take it. Plus, knowing my mother, she'll want a big wedding, which will take a while to plan. So the earliest we could set the date would be autumn. Maybe early November."

"I was hoping for a quiet wedding on the beach just before dawn with our parents and close friends. Preferably next month sometime," Peter said.

"Next month?" Gilly choked. "We can't do that. My mother would never forgive me."

"I thought it was me you were marrying, not your mother," grumbled Peter.

Setting the palms of her hands on the

tabletop, Gilly half rose from her seat and glared jokingly at Peter. "Are you trying to pick a fight already?" she asked with a saucy grin.

"It's my wedding, too," Peter challenged. "I think, in the interest of fairness to your future husband, you should consider my ideas."

Gilly mumbled something under her breath, and reached for the potato salad.

Holding back a smile, Elizabeth glanced at Breed, who seemed to be enjoying the moment. She felt as if she could read his thoughts, and she agreed. Gilly and Peter fought much more now that they were in love.

They finished their meal, then got serious about setting up camp.

"I'll unload Hilda," Breed said as he stood.

"I'll help," Peter offered, pointing to Gilly. "The wedding will be next month, on the beach at sunrise."

"Thanks for the invitation, big shot. I hope I can make it."

"I'm doing the dishes," Elizabeth reminded them, and she hurriedly swallowed the last bite of her meal. Everyone was suddenly busy, and she didn't want to sit idle.

The paper plates were easily disposed of in a garbage container. She placed the potato salad and other leftovers in the cooler. The only items left were the plastic forks and a single saucepan.

With a dish towel draped around her neck, and the plasticware, liquid soap and rag dumped inside the saucepan, she headed toward the creek she'd discovered with Breed.

"Hey, where are you going?" Gilly called out as Elizabeth left.

"To wash these." She held up the pan. "I'll be right back. Breed said something about taking a hike."

Gilly's smile was crooked. "Yes, but I

think he was referring to me and Peter. If we don't quit fighting, I have the feeling we may have to walk home."

Elizabeth located the stream without a problem and knelt on the soft earth beside the water, humming as she rubbed the rag along the inside of the aluminum pan. A flash of color caught her attention, and she glanced upward. A deer was poised in a meadow on the other side of the water. Mesmerized, she watched the wild creature with a powerful sense of awe and appreciation.

Slowly, she straightened, afraid her movements would frighten off the lovely animal. But the doe merely raised its regal head, and she stared into its beautiful dark eyes. The animal didn't appear to be frightened by her presence.

Wondering how close she could get, she crossed the burbling water, stepping carefully from one stone to another. When she reached the other side, the doe was gone. Disappointed, she walked to the spot where the animal had been standing and saw that it had gone farther into the forest, and now was barely visible. She decided to follow it, thinking she might be able to catch a glimpse of a fawn. She wished she'd thought to bring her camera. But she hadn't expected to see anything like this.

Keeping a safe distance, she followed the deer, rather proud of her ability to track it. She realized that the animal wasn't trying to escape or she wouldn't have had a chance of following it this far.

The lovely creature paused, and she took the opportunity to rest on a felled tree while keeping an eye on the deer. A glance at her watch told her that she'd been away from camp almost an hour. She didn't want to worry anyone, so even though the chase was fun, she felt forced to abandon it. With bittersweet regret, she stood and gave a waving salute to her beautiful friend.

An hour later, she owned up to the fact that she was lost. The taste of panic filled her mouth, and she took several deep breaths to calm herself.

"Help!" she screamed, as loudly as she could. Her voice echoed through the otherwise silent forest. "I'm here!" she cried out, a frantic edge to her words. Hurrying now, she half ran through the thick woods until she stumbled and caught herself against a bush. A thorny limb caught on the flesh of her upper arm and lightly gouged her skin.

Elizabeth yelped with pain and grabbed at her wound. When her fingers came away sticky with blood, a sickening sensation attacked her stomach.

"Calm down," she told herself out loud, thinking the sound of her own voice would have a soothing effect. It didn't, and she paused again to force herself to breathe evenly.

"Breed, oh, Breed," she whispered as she moved through the dense cover, holding her arm. "Please find me. Please, please find me."

Her legs felt weak, and her lungs burned with the effort to push on. Every step cost her more than the previous one.

She tried to force the terror from her mind and concentrate on happy thoughts. The memory of her mother's laughter took the edge of exertion from her steps. The long walks with Breed along the beach. She recalled their first argument and how she'd insisted that she could find the way back. Without him, she would have been lost then, too. His words from that night echoed in her tired mind. *If you ever get lost, promise me you'll stay in one place.* She stumbled to an abrupt halt and looked around her. Nothing was familiar. She could be going in the opposite direction from the campground for all she knew. She was dreadfully tired and growing weaker every minute, the level of her remaining endurance dropping with each step.

If she was going to stop, she decided, she would find a place where she could sit and rest. She found a patch of moss that grew beside a tree and lowered herself to a sitting position. Her breath was uneven and ragged, but she suspected it was more from fear than anything.

Someone would find her soon, she told herself. Soon. The word repeated in her mind a thousand times, offering hope.

Every minute seemed an hour and every hour a month as she sat and waited. When the sun began to set, she realized she would probably be spending the night in the woods. The thought couldn't frighten her any more than she was already. At least not until darkness settled over the forest.

Not once did she doze or even try to sleep, afraid she would miss a light or the sound of a voice. Tears filled her eyes

at the darkest part of the night that pre-
ceded dawn and she realized she could
die out here. At least, she was convinced,
her mother was waiting for her on the
other side of life.

Of course, she had regrets—lots of
them. Things she had wanted to do in
her lifetime. But her biggest regret was
that she had never told Breed how much
she loved him.

She stood up gratefully when the sun
came over the horizon, its golden rays
bathing the earth with its warmth. She
was so cold. For a time she had been
convinced she would freeze. Her teeth
had chattered, and she'd huddled into a
tight ball, believing this night would be
her last.

Her stomach growled, and her tongue
had grown thick with the need for water.
For a long time she debated whether
she should strike out again and look for
something to drink or stay where she

was. Every muscle protested when she decided to search out water, and she quickly sat back down, amazed at how weak she had become.

She tried to call out, but her voice refused to cooperate, and even the attempt to shout took more energy than she could muster.

With her eyes closed, her back supported by the tree trunk, she strained her ears for the slightest sound. The day before, while walking with Breed, she had thought the woods were quiet and serene. Now she was astonished at the cacophony that surrounded her. The loud squawk of birds and the rustle of branches in the breeze filled the forest. And then there were the other noises she couldn't identify.

"Beth." Her name echoed from faraway, barely audible.

With a reserve of energy she hadn't known she possessed, Elizabeth leaped

to her feet and screamed back. "Here...
I'm here!" Certain they would never
hear her, she ran frantically toward the
sound of the voice, crying as she pushed
branches out of her way. They would
search in another area if she couldn't
make herself heard. She couldn't bear it
if she had come so close to being found
only to be left behind.

"Here!" she cried again and again,
until her voice was hardly more than a
whisper.

Breed saw her before she saw him.
"Thank God," he said, and the sound of
it reached her. She turned and saw the
torment leave his face as he covered the
distance between them with giant strides.

Fiercely, she was hauled into his arms
as he buried his face in her neck. A shud-
der ran through him as she wrapped her
arms around him and started to weep
with relief. Huge tears of happiness
rolled down her face, making wet tracks

in the dust that had settled on her cheeks. She was so relieved that she didn't notice the other men with Breed until he released her.

Some of the previous agony returned to Breed's eyes as he ran his finger down the dried blood that had crusted on her upper arm.

A forest ranger handed her a canteen of water and told her to take small sips. Another man spoke into a walkie-talkie, advising the members of the search party that she had been found and was safe.

The trip back to camp was hazy in Elizabeth's memory. Questions came at her from every direction. She answered them as best she could and apologized profusely for all the trouble she had caused.

The only thing that stood out in her mind was how far she had wandered. It seemed hours before they reached the campground. Breed took over at that point, taking her in his arms and carrying her into the tent.

The next thing she knew, she was awake and darkness surrounded her. She sat up and glanced around. Gilly lay sleeping on one side of her, Breed on the other. Peter was beside Gilly.

Breed's eyes opened, and he sat up with her. "How do you feel?" he whispered.

"A whole lot better. Is there anything to eat? I'm starved."

He took her hand and helped her out of the sleeping bag. Sitting her at the picnic table, he rummaged around and returned with a plate heaped with food.

He took a seat across the table from her—to gaze upon her unspoiled beauty, he told her, laughing. A lantern that hung from a tree dimly lit the area surrounding the tent and table. His features were bloodless, so pale that she felt a surge of guilt at her thoughtlessness.

She set her fork aside. "Breed, I'm so sorry. Can you forgive me?"

He wiped a hand across his face and didn't answer immediately. "I've never been so happy to see freckles in my life."

"You look terrible."

He answered her with a weak smile. "You're a brave woman, Beth. A lot of people would have panicked."

"Don't think I didn't," she told him with a shaky laugh. "There were a few hours there last night when I was sure that I'd die in those woods." She glanced lovingly at him. "The craziest part of it was that I kept thinking of all the things I regret not having done in my life."

"I suppose that's only natural."

"Do you want to know what I regretted the most?"

"What?" he asked with a tired sigh, supporting his forehead with the palms of his hands, not looking at her.

"I kept thinking how sorry I was that I'd never told you how much I love you."

Slowly, Breed raised his gaze to hers. The look in his tired amber eyes became brilliant as he studied her.

"Well, say something," she pleaded, rubbing a hand across her forehead. "I probably would have told you long ago except that I was afraid the same thing would happen to me as happened to Gilly." She paused and inhaled a deep, wobbly breath. "I know you love me in your own way, but I—"

"In my own way?" Breed returned harshly. "I love you so much that if we hadn't found you in those woods I would have stayed out there until I died, looking for you." He got up from the picnic table and walked around to her. "You asked me if I can forgive you. The answer is yes. But I don't think my heart has recovered yet. We're bound to have one crazy married life together, I can tell you that.

I don't think I can take many more of your adventures."

"Married life…?" she repeated achingly.

Breed didn't answer her with words, only hauled her into his arms and held on to her as if he couldn't bear to let her go.

"If this is a dream, don't wake me," she said.

"My love is no fantasy. This is reality."

"Oh, Breed," she whispered as tears of happiness clouded her eyes. She slipped her arms around his neck and pressed her face into his strong, muscular chest.

"Are we going to argue like Peter and Gilly? Or can we have a quiet ceremony with family and a few friends?"

She brushed his lips with a featherlight kiss. "Anything you say."

"Aren't you agreeable!"

She curled tighter in his embrace. "Just promise to love me no matter what." She was thinking of what his reaction would be to her family's wealth and social position. He had a right to know, but telling him now would ruin the magic of the moment. As for not having said anything in the past, she was pleased that she hadn't. Breed loved her for herself. Money and all that it could buy hadn't influenced his feelings. Maybe she was anticipating trouble for no reason.

His smile broadened. The radiant light in his amber eyes kindled a soft glow of happiness in her. His fingers explored her neck and shoulders, holding her so close that for a moment it was impossible to breathe normally. When he moved to kiss her, she slid her hands over his muscular chest and linked them behind his neck. He allowed her only small gasps of air before a new shiver of excitement stole her breath completely.

Her parted lips were trembling and swollen from Breed's plundering kisses when he finally groaned, pulled himself away and sat up straight. "I think the sooner we arrange the wedding, the better." He sighed. "I'd prefer a tent built for two." He ran a hand over his eyes. "And this may be old-fashioned, but I'd like to be married when we start our family."

Elizabeth knew the music in her heart would never fade. Not with this man. He didn't sound old-fashioned to her but refreshingly wonderful.

"I'm so glad you want children." Her voice throbbed with the beat of her heart.

"A houseful, at least." His husky voice betrayed the tight rein he held on his needs. "But for now I'd be content to start with a wedding ring."

"Soon," she promised.

"Tomorrow we'll go down and get the license."

"Tomorrow?" The immediacy frightened her. She wanted to get married, but she couldn't see the necessity of rushing into it quite *that* quickly.

"Maybe we should pack up and drive to Reno and get married immediately."

"No." Elizabeth didn't know why she felt so strongly about that. "I want to stand before God to make my vows, not the Last Chance Hitching Post."

She could see Breed's smile. "You're sure you want to marry me?" he said.

In response, she leaned over and teased him with her lips. "You'll never need to doubt my love," she said, and playfully nipped at his earlobe.

"Who would have believed you'd get lost in the woods?" Gilly commented late the next night as they unpacked the camping gear in the apartment kitchen.

"Who would have believed we'd both become engaged in one weekend?"

"Elizabeth, I can't tell you how frantic we all were," Gilly said tightly. "Breed was like a man possessed. When you didn't come back, he went to find you. When he didn't return, Peter and I went to look for you both."

Color heated Elizabeth's face. "I was so stupid." Her inexperience had ruined their trip. After a good night's sleep, they'd packed up and headed straight back to San Francisco.

"Don't be so hard on yourself. This was your first time camping. You didn't know."

"But I feel so terrible for being such an idiot."

Gilly straightened and brushed the hair off her forehead. "Thank God you're safe," she said, staring into the distance. "I don't know what would have happened to Breed if we hadn't found you. Beth, he was like a madman. I don't think there was anyone who didn't realize that Breed would have died in the attempt to find you."

Leaning against the counter, Elizabeth

expelled a painful sigh. "On the bright side of things, getting lost has done a lot for Breed and me. I wonder how long it would have been otherwise before we admitted how we felt."

"It's taken too long as it is. I knew almost from the beginning that you two were meant for each other."

Elizabeth attempted to disguise a smile. "We don't all have your insight, I guess."

Gilly seemed unaware of the teasing glint in her roommate's eye. "Peter's coming to get me in a few minutes. We're going to go talk to my parents. Will you be safe all by yourself, or should I phone Breed?"

"He's coming over in a while. I'm cooking dinner."

Breed arrived five minutes after Gilly left with Peter. He kissed her lightly on the cheek. "How do you feel?"

"Hungry," she said with a warm smile. "Let's get this show on the road."

"I thought you were cooking me dinner."

"I am. But we left the food in Hilda, which means it's at your place. If I'm going to share my life with you, then the least you can do is introduce me to your kitchen."

That uneasy look came over his features again. "We could go out just as well."

"Breed," Elizabeth intoned dramatically, "how many times do we have to argue about this apartment of yours? It's so obvious you don't want me there."

His mouth tightened grimly. "Let's go. I don't want another argument."

"Well, that's encouraging."

The brisk walk took them about fifteen minutes. His apartment was exactly as she remembered it. No pictures or knickknacks that marked the place as his. That continued to confuse her, but she couldn't believe that he would hide anything from her.

There wasn't much to work with left from their trip, and his cupboards were bare, but she assumed this was because he ate most of his meals out.

"Spaghetti's my specialty," she told him as she tied a towel around her waist.

"That sounds good."

He hovered at her elbow as she sautéed the meat and stood at her side while she chopped the vegetables. He shadowed her every action, and when she couldn't tolerate his brand of "togetherness" another second, she turned and ushered him into the living room.

"Read the paper or something, will you? You're driving me crazy."

His eyes showed his indecision. He glanced back into the kitchen, then nodded as he reached for the newspaper.

Singing softly as she worked, Elizabeth mentally reviewed her cooking lessons from school. The sauce was simmering and the pasta was boiling. She decided to set the table. A few loose papers and mail littered the countertop. Humming cheerfully, she moved them to his desk on the far side of the kitchen. The top of the desk was cluttered with more papers. As she set down his mail, she noticed a legal-looking piece of paper. She continued to hum as idly she glanced at it and realized it was a gun permit. *Breed carried a gun.* A chill shot up her spine. The song died on her lips. Breed and firearms seemed as incongruous as mixing oil and water. She would ask him about it later.

"Anything I can do?" he volunteered, seeming to have relaxed now.

"Open the wine."

"Wine?"

"You mean you don't have any?" she asked as she stirred the pasta. "The flavors in my sauce will be incomplete without the complement of wine."

"I take it you want me to buy us a bottle."

"You got it."

"Okay, let's go." He stood and tucked in his shirttails.

"Me? I can't go now. I've got to drain the pasta and finish setting the table."

He hesitated.

"Honestly, Breed, there's a grocery just down the street. You don't need me to hold your hand."

He didn't look pleased about it, but he turned and walked out.

The minute the door was closed, Elizabeth returned to his desk. She knew she was snooping, but the gun permit puzzled her, and she wanted to look it over. The permit listed a different address, confirming her suspicions that he hadn't been in this apartment long. The paper felt like it was burning her fingers, and she set it aside, hating the way her curiosity had gotten in the way of her better judgment.

She could ask him, of course, but she felt uneasy about that. Where would he keep a lethal weapon in this bare place? She wondered about the kind of gun he carried. With her index finger she pulled out the top desk drawer. It wasn't in sight, but a notebook with her full name written across the top caught her gaze. Fascinated, she pulled it from the drawer and flipped it open. Page after page of meticulous notes detailed her comings and goings, her habits and her friends. *Breed had been following her since she arrived!* But whatever for? This was bizarre.

Coiled tightness gripped her throat as she pulled open another drawer. Hurt and anger and a thousand terrifying emotions she had never thought to experience with regard to Breed filled her senses. The drawer was filled with correspondence with her father. Andrew Breed had been hired by her family as her bodyguard.

Nine

Elizabeth backed away from the drawer. Her hand was pressed against her breast as the blood drained from her face. Her heart was pounding wildly in her ears, and for several seconds she was unable to breathe. So many inconsistencies about Breed fell into place. She was amazed that she could have been so blind, so utterly stupid. His cover had been perfect. Dating her had simplified his job immeasurably.

Her stomach rolled, and she knew she was going to be sick. She closed the drawer and staggered into the bathroom. It was there that Breed found her.

"Beth." His voice was filled with concern. "You look terrible."

She didn't meet his eyes. "I'm…I'm all right. I just need a moment."

He placed his arm across her back, and the touch, although light, seemed to burn through the material of her shirt, branding her. Leading her into the living room, he sat her down on the sofa and brought in a cool rag.

"I was afraid something like this might happen," he murmured solicitously. "You're probably having a delayed reaction to the trauma of this weekend."

She closed her eyes and nodded, still unable to look at him. "I want to go home." Somehow the words managed to slip past the stranglehold she felt around her throat.

Not until they were ready to leave did she glance out Breed's window and realize that, thanks to the city's hills, her apartment could be seen from his. No wonder he was able to document her whereabouts so accurately. Mr. Andrew Breed was a clever man, deceptive and more devious than she could have dreamed. And he excelled at his job. She didn't try to fool herself. She was a job to him and little or nothing more than that.

It was no small wonder he'd suggested they go to Reno and get married right away. He wanted the deed accomplished before they confronted her father. He knew what her family would say if she were to marry a bodyguard. Her emotions when her purse had been taken had been a small-scale version of what she felt now. A part of her inner self had been violated. But the pain went far deeper. Deep enough to sear her soul. She doubted that she would ever be the same again.

Concerned, Breed helped her on with

her sweater and gripped her elbow. Several times during the short drive to her apartment he glanced her way, a worried look marring his handsome face. After he had unlocked her apartment and helped her into her room, she changed clothes, took a sleeping pill and climbed into bed. But the pill didn't work. She lay awake with a lump the size of a grapefruit blocking her throat. Every swallow hurt. Crying might have helped, but no tears would come.

She didn't know how long she lay staring at the shadows on the ceiling. The front door clicked open, and she heard Breed whisper to Gilly. She was mildly surprised that he'd stayed, then grinned sarcastically. Of course he would; he'd been paid to baby-sit her. And knowing her father, the fee had been generous.

The front door clicked again, and she heard Gilly assure Breed that she would take care of Elizabeth. The words were almost ludicrous. These two people whom she'd come to love this summer had given her so much. But they had taken away even more. No, she thought. She didn't blame Gilly. She was grateful to have had her as a friend. Gilly might have been in on this scheme, but she doubted it.

Finally Elizabeth heard Gilly go into her bedroom. An hour later, convinced her friend would be asleep, she silently pushed back the covers and climbed out of bed. Dragging her suitcases from the closet, she quickly and quietly emptied her drawers and hangers. She only took what she had brought with her from Boston. Everything else she was leaving for her roommate.

The apartment key and a note to Gilly were left propped against a vase on the kitchen table. A sad smile touched Elizabeth's pale features as she set a second note, addressed to Breed, beside the first.

She picked it up and read over the simple message again. It read: *The game's over. You lose.*

The taxi ride to the airport seemed to take hours. Elizabeth kept looking over her shoulder, afraid Breed was following. She didn't want to think of how many times this summer he had done exactly that. The thought made her more determined than ever to get away.

There wasn't a plane scheduled to leave for Boston until the next morning, so she took the red-eye to New York. Luckily, the wait was less than two hours. Her greatest fear was that Gilly would wake up and go to check on her. Finding her gone, she would be sure to contact Breed.

Restlessly, Elizabeth walked around the airport. She knew that she would never forget this city. The cable cars, the sounds and smells of Fisherman's Wharf, sailing, the beach… Her musings did a buzzing tailspin. No, thoughts of San Francisco would always be irrevocably tied to Breed. She wanted to hate him, but she couldn't. He'd given her happy memories, and she would struggle to keep those untainted by the mud of his deception.

The flight was uneventful. The first-class section had only one other traveler, a businessman who worked out of his briefcase the entire time.

Even though it was only 10:00 a.m. when her plane landed, New York was sweltering in an August heat wave. The limousine delivered her to the St. Moritz, a fashionable uptown hotel that was situated across the street from Central Park South.

Exhausted, she took a hot shower and fell asleep almost immediately afterward in the air-conditioned room.

When she awoke, it was nearly dinner-time. Although she hadn't eaten anything in twenty-four hours, she wasn't hungry.

A walk in Central Park lifted her from the well of overwhelming self-pity. She bought a pretzel and squirted thick yellow mustard over it. As she lazily strolled beside the pond, goldfish the size of trout came to the water's edge, anticipating a share of her meal. Not wanting to disappoint them, she broke off a piece of the doughy pretzel and tossed it into the huge pond.

A young bearded man, strumming a ballad on his guitar, sat on a green bench looking for handouts. She placed a five-dollar bill in the open guitar case.

"Thanks, lady," he sang, and returned her wave with a bob of his dark head.

Most of the park benches were occupied by a wide range of people from all walks of life. She had taken a two-day trip to the Big Apple the previous year and stayed at the St. Moritz, but she hadn't gone into Central Park. The thought hadn't entered her mind.

Today she strolled around the pond, hoping that the sights and sounds of the vibrant city would ease the heaviness in her heart. Unfamiliar settings filled with anonymous faces were no longer intimidating. San Francisco had done that for her.

An hour later she stepped into the cool hotel room and sighed. Reaching for the phone, she dialed Boston.

"Hello, Dad," she said when he picked up, her voice devoid of emotion.

"Elizabeth, where are you?" he demanded instantly.

"New York."

"Why in heaven's name did you run off like that?"

His question drew a faint smile. "I think you already know why," she answered softly, resignedly. "How often have you hired men to watch me in the past?"

"Did he tell you?" her father responded brusquely.

"No. I found out on my own."

"The fool," he issued harshly under his breath.

She disagreed. The only fool in this situation had been herself, for falling in love with Breed.

A strained silence stretched along the wires.

"How often, Dad?" she finally asked.

"Only a few," he answered after a long moment.

"But why?" she asked, exhaling forcefully. The pain of the knowledge was physical as well as mental. Her stomach ached, and she lowered herself into the upholstered wing chair in her suite and leaned forward to rest her elbows on her knees.

"That's a subject we shouldn't discuss over the phone. I want you at home."

"There are a lot of things *I* want, too," she returned in a shallow whisper.

"Elizabeth, please. Be reasonable."

"Give me a few days," she insisted. "I need time to think."

Her father began to argue. She closed her eyes and listened for a few moments. Then she whispered, "Goodbye, Dad," and hung up.

The next morning she checked out of the hotel, rented a car and headed north. Setting a leisurely pace, she stopped along the way to enjoy the beauty of the Atlantic Ocean. It took her three days to drive home.

She recognized that her father would consider her actions immature, but for her, this time alone with her thoughts had been vital. The long drive, the magnificent coastline, the solitude, gave her the necessary time to come to terms with her father's actions. Decisions were made. Although her father hadn't asked for it, she gave him her forgiveness. He had only been doing what he thought was best.

The thing that shocked her most had been her own stupidity. How could she have been so gullible? All the evidence of Breed's deceit had been there, but she had been blinded by her love. But no more. Never again. Loving someone only caused emotional pain. She had been naive and incredibly foolish.

She wouldn't allow her father to interfere in her life that way again. Once she got home, she would make arrangements to find a place of her own. Breaking away had been long overdue. This summer she'd proved to her father and herself that she was capable of holding a job. And that was what she decided to do: get a job. She spoke fluent French, and enough German and Italian to make her last visit to Europe trouble-free. Surely there was something she could do with those skills.

Not once during the drive home did she allow bitterness to tarnish her memories of Breed. Ultimately, the special relationship they'd shared led to heartache. But she was grateful to him for the precious gift that he'd so unwittingly given her.

One thing she couldn't accept was his calculated deception. Maybe forgiveness would come later, but right now the pain cut so deep that she knew it would take a long time, and maybe it would never come.

It was midafternoon when she pulled up in front of the huge family home.

The white-haired butler opened the door and gave her a stiff but genuine smile.

"Welcome home, Miss Elizabeth." His head dipped slightly as he spoke.

"Hello, Bently."

"Your father's been expecting you, miss. You're to go directly to the library."

Although he hadn't said as much, she knew he was warning her that her father wasn't pleased.

"I'll see to your luggage," he continued.

"Thank you, Bently."

Her elderly ally inclined his head in silent understanding.

Elizabeth stood in the great entry hall and looked around with new eyes. The house was magnificent, a showpiece, but it felt cold and unwelcoming. The heart of this home had died with her mother.

Knocking politely against the polished mahogany door that reached from the ceiling to the floor, Elizabeth waited with calm deliberation.

Charles Wainwright's reply was curt and impatient. "Come in."

"Hello, Father," she said as she walked through the door.

"Elizabeth." He raised himself out of his chair. Relief relaxed the tightness in his weathered brow and he gave her a brief, perfunctory hug. "Now, what's all this nonsense of needing time away?"

She was saved from having to reply by the arrival of Helene. The maid seemed to appear noiselessly, carrying a silver tray with a coffeepot and two delicate china cups.

Both Elizabeth and her father waited to resume their conversation until Helene had left the room.

"I have a few unanswered questions of my own," she said as she stood and dutifully filled the first cup. She handed it to her father. Charles Wainwright's hair was completely white now, she noted as he accepted the steaming cup from her hand. Once, a long time past, her father's hair had been the same sandy shade as her own. The famous Wainwright blond good looks. Charlie was dark like her mother. But other than her coloring, Elizabeth felt as if she had nothing in common with this man. He wasn't affectionate. She couldn't ever recall him bouncing her on his knee or telling her stories when she was a child. The only time she recalled seeing deep emotion from him had been after her mother's funeral.

Her reverie was interrupted by coffee that dripped from the spout of the silver service and scalded her fingertips. She managed to set the pot aside before giving an involuntary gasp of surprise. Tears filled her eyes, but not from physical pain.

"Elizabeth." Charles Wainwright leapt to his feet. "You've burned yourself." He turned aside. "Helene!" he shouted. Elizabeth couldn't remember hearing that much emotion in his voice for a long time. "Bring the first-aid kit."

"I'm fine," she struggled to reassure him between sudden sobs. She hadn't wept when she learned of Breed's deceit. Nor had she revealed her grief at her mother's funeral. After all, she was a Wainwright, and tears were a sign of weakness. Now she was home, with possibly the only person alive who loved her for herself, and they sat like polite acquaintances, sharing coffee and shielding their hearts. A dam within her burst, and she began to sob uncontrollably.

She could see by the concerned look on his face that her father didn't know how to react. He raised and lowered his hands, impotently unsure of himself. Finally he circled his arms around her and patted her gently on the back as if he were afraid she was a fragile porcelain doll that would break.

"Princess," he whispered, "what is it?"

Helene burst in the door, and Charles dismissed her with a wave of his hand.

"Who's hurt you?"

Between a fresh wave of sobs, she shook her head.

Her father handed her his starched and pressed linen handkerchief, and she held it to her eyes.

"My dear," he said, smoothing her back. "You have the look of a woman in love."

"No." She pulled free of his loose embrace and violently shook her head. "I can't love him after what he's done," she choked out between sobs.

"And what did he do?"

She sniffled. "Nothing. I...can't talk about it. Not now," she whispered in painful denial. "I apologize for acting like an idiot. I'll go upstairs and lie down for an hour or so, and I'll be fine."

"Princess, are you sure you won't tell me?"

Fresh tears squeezed through her

damp lashes. "Not now." She turned toward the great hall. "Dad," she said with her back to him, "I'll probably be leaving for Europe within the week."

Her father was silent for a moment. "Running away won't solve anything." His haunting voice, gentle with wisdom, followed her as she left the library.

One suitcase was packed and another half-filled. She'd realized after one night that she couldn't remain in this house. Once the tears had come, the aching loneliness in her heart had throbbed with its intensity. Her father was right when he told her running away wouldn't heal the void. But escaping came naturally; she had been doing it for so long. Last night she hadn't gone down to dinner, and she'd been shocked when her father brought her a tray later in the evening. She had pretended to be asleep.

She regretted that now, and decided to go downstairs and say goodbye to him.

Tucking her passport in her purse, she examined the contents of her suitcases one last time before securing the locks and leaving them outside her door. The reservations for her flight had been made earlier that morning, and plenty of time remained before she needed to leave for the airport. But already she was restless. Forcing a smile on her pale features, she descended the stairs.

She was only halfway down the staircase when she heard Bently engaged in a heated argument with someone at the front door. The other voice was achingly familiar. Breed.

That he was angry and impatient was apparent as his raised voice echoed through the hall. She took another step, and then her father appeared in the foyer.

"That'll be all, Bently," her father said with calm authority. "I'll see Mr. Breed."

She restrained a gasp and drew closer to the banister. Clearly neither man was aware of her presence.

Breed stepped into the house. His deeply tanned features were set in hard lines as he approached her father.

"I appreciate the fact that you're seeing me." His voice was laced with heavy sarcasm. "But I can assure you that I was prepared to wait as long as it took."

"After four days of pounding down my door, I can believe that's a fair assumption," her father retorted stiffly. "But now that you have my attention, what is it you want?"

"Elizabeth," Breed said without hesitation. "Where is she?"

"Your job of protecting my daughter was terminated when she left San Francisco. I believe you've received your check."

She watched, fascinated and shocked, as Breed took an envelope from his pocket and ripped it in two. "I don't want a dime of this money. I told you that before, and I'm telling you again."

"You earned it."

Every damn penny, Elizabeth wanted to shout at him.

"I kept my word, Wainwright," Breed explained forcefully. "I didn't tell Beth a thing. But I hated every minute of this assignment, and you knew it."

"Why? I thought this type of work was your specialty. You came highly recommended," her father said quietly.

Breed rubbed a hand across his eyes, and she knew the torment she saw in his features was mirrored in her own. When he lowered his hand, he must have caught a glimpse of her from out of the corner of his eye. He hesitated and turned toward her.

"Beth." He said her name softly, as though he was afraid she would disappear again. He moved to the foot of the stairs. The tightness eased from his face as he stared up at her.

"Mr. Wainwright," Breed said, and the anger was gone from his voice as he glanced briefly at her father, "I love your daughter."

"No," Elizabeth said in agitation. "You don't know the meaning of the word. I was nothing more than a lucrative business proposition."

Breed pulled another envelope from his shirt and handed it to her father. His eyes left her only briefly. "While we're on the subject of money…"

Her gaze wavered under the blazing force of his.

"This paper proves that I'm not a poor man. I own a thousand acres of prime California timberland. The land has been in my family for a hundred years," Breed stated evenly, then turned toward her father. "I have no need of the Wainwright money. From the first day I met your daughter, it's stood between us like a brick wall."

He turned back to the stairs, and his look grew gentle. "I love you, Beth Wainwright. I've loved you from the moment we went swimming and I saw you for the wonderful woman you are."

Her heart was crying out for her to run to Breed. But the feelings of betrayal and hurt kept her rooted to the stairs. Her hand curved around the polished banister until she was sure her fingernails would dent the wood.

At her silence, he returned his attention to her father. "Mr. Wainwright, I'm asking for your permission to marry your daughter—"

"I won't marry you," she interrupted in angry protest. "You lied to me. All those weeks you—"

"You weren't exactly honest with me," he returned levelly. "And there was ample opportunity for you to explain everything. You have no right to be mad at me." He paused, and the hardness left his chiseled features. "I'll say it again. I love you, Beth. I want you to share my life."

Indecision played across her face, and her gaze met her father's. Breed's eyes followed hers, and a proud look stole over them.

"I'm asking for your permission, Wainwright," Breed said coolly. "But I'll be honest. I plan to marry your daughter with or without it."

A hint of mirth brightened her father's face. "That's a brash statement, young man."

"Daddy!" Elizabeth called, knowing what her father would say to someone like Breed. Her heart and her pride waged a desperate battle.

Charles Wainwright ignored his daughter. "As it is, I realize that Elizabeth loves you. I may be a crusty old man, but I'm not too blind to see that you'll make her happy. You have my permission, Andrew Breed. Fill this house with grandchildren and bring some laughter into its halls again."

Breed appeared as stunned as Elizabeth.

"Go on." Charles Wainwright flicked his wrist in the direction of his daughter. "And don't take no for an answer."

"I have no intention of doing so," Breed said as he climbed the stairs two at a time.

Elizabeth felt the crazy desire to turn and run, but she stayed where she was, her body motionless with indecision. She bit into her trembling bottom lip as her pride surrendered the first battle.

"Your money will go into a trust fund for our children, Beth," Breed began with a frown. "I don't want a penny of what's yours. There's only one thing I'm after."

"What's that?" she asked in a quiet

murmur, battling with the potency of his nearness.

He slid his hands around her waist and pulled her into the circle of his arms. "A wife."

Her breath came in small flutters as he lowered his mouth and paused a scant inch above hers. Their breath merged. She swayed against him, her hands moving over his chest. The entire time her pride urged her to break free and walk away. But her heart held her steadfast.

"Don't fight me so hard," he whispered, claiming her lips in a kiss so tender that she melted against him.

"Together we'll build a lumber kingdom," he whispered into her hair.

"I don't know," she faltered. "I need time to think. I'm confused." She wanted him so much. It was her pride speaking, not her heart.

"Elizabeth," her father called from the hall. "I think it's only fair to tell you that your Andrew came to me a few weeks back and asked to be relieved of this case. Naturally, I declined and demanded that he maintain his anonymity."

Her eyes met Breed's. "Your business trip?"

He nodded and placed his hands on her shoulders. "Is it really so difficult to decide?" he asked in a husky whisper.

She stared at the familiar features and saw the pain carved in them. "No, not at all."

For a breathless moment they looked at one another.

Then Elizabeth's pride surrendered to her heart as she pressed her mouth to his.

* * * * *

Name	(PLEASE PRINT)	

Address		Apt. #

City	State/Prov.	Zip/Postal Code

Signature (if under 18, a parent or guardian must sign)

Mail to the **Harlequin® Reader Service:**

IN U.S.A.: P.O. Box 1867, Buffalo, NY 14240-1867
IN CANADA: P.O. Box 609, Fort Erie, Ontario L2A 5X3